D1522220

TWIST

OF

TRUTH

A contemporary murder mystery

DIANE M DICKSON

THE
BOOK
FOLKS

Paperback edition published by

The Book Folks

London, 2017

ISBN 978-1-5205-4790-9

www.thebookfolks.com

For my family, who keep me grounded.

Chapter 1

Nothing had changed. Simon stepped down from the coach and slung the backpack onto his left shoulder. Heavy grey cloud spilled a dull drizzle onto the old flagstones of the High Street. Puddles of light reflecting the shop windows might have looked pretty if the pavement hadn't been splattered with old chewing gum, wet paper, take away cartons and dissolving dog shit. He sighed and turned to watch the National Express bus pull away. He felt a pull of longing, he should have stayed on, warm and drowsy in the stale air.

A small blue car swooshed past, splattering his trousers with filthy water and soaking the insides of his leather shoes. "Yeah, welcome home." He muttered under his breath and flipped two fingers after the mindless driver, then took the first steps into his past.

There was no trouble remembering the way, he had walked this route back and forth every day for years. First to the old, stone-built school and then later to work. The names on the shops might have changed but the streets were the same, High Street, Bradford Road, Church Street. An odd feeling overtook him, he knew he was older, stiffer in his shoulders and scarred about his face but inside he was the boy, the youth, the young man; all together they sat in his memory and watched as he climbed the hill towards the church, rounded the corner into Faith Street and came to a halt beside the blue wooden gate, still swinging on creaky hinges. He flung it back and stepped forward to the two-up two-down terraced house.

The door was different, the scarred wooden one had been replaced with white plastic sporting a fan-shaped window. There was a bell push on the frame. His stomach flipped as he raised his finger.

He could hear it sounding deep inside the house, a harsh metallic rattle. He pushed once and leaned back, scanning the upstairs windows. There was no sign of life from inside, no shadow wavered behind the coloured glass, no dog barked. There was always a dog, a pain of a dog that chewed what it should leave alone, shed hair on the furniture and clothes alike and barked when someone knocked on the door, no bell, no bell back then. No dog now. He was relieved as he turned away and trod back down the crumbling concrete path. He had done what was right, what was expected and now he could walk away.

Right or left at the gate, did it matter? He turned right mainly because before he had usually turned left. Some of the houses had new windows, blinds instead of net curtains, paved front gardens with cars squeezed into spaces too small for the bulk of them. He thought it felt more affluent, but then how would he know, what did he have to compare this with?

The rain was heavier and he was cold and thirsty.

The changes at the Hope and Anchor were more obvious, there were tables outside, an untidy line of them with chairs tipped to stop the rain puddling on plastic seats. The ground was littered with soggy cigarette butts. When he pushed through the door he saw an open area, no snug and bar as it was in his memory, just a broad space filled with dark oak and smelling of vinegar, hot fat and cleaning fluid. He threw his bag down in front of the bar and slid onto a tall stool.

The young woman pushed away from the shelf she was leaning on and looked at him, unsmiling. She didn't know just how special this was. "Pint of bitter please love." With a nod she moved along the bar, grabbed a glass and began to draw his pint. The polished wood and brass pumps had gone. She flipped up a small tap and the tawny liquid poured. The girl was disinterested but efficient and the beer placed in front of him was clear with a foamy head, bubbles surging upwards. "Two fifty."

"Sorry?"

"Two fifty, or was there sommat else?"

"No, no it's just – no it's fine sorry, miles away." He dug into his pocket and rooted among the change, he handed over three pound coins. "That's okay love." She looked down at the money and raised her eyebrows. "Right, ta."

For a wild moment he was swept with panic, how could he do this? When he had climbed down from the bus he thought nothing had changed but now he was beginning to see that in truth everything had.

He reached for the heavy glass and curled his fingers around it feeling the cool, the smooth hardness, the weight of it. He licked his lips, and took the first swallow, felt the foam on his lip, the liquid in his throat and the richness of malt and hops on his tongue. This at least was all it should be, all he had hoped, and he was astounded to feel the sting in his eyes as the images flooded in, filling dark spaces in his memory.

When he had finished the first long drink he wiped his damp mouth with the back of a hand and glanced around. The late afternoon pub was quiet. There was no jukebox in the corner, instead a huge television mounted on the wall flashed a football game with scrolling commentary sliding unread along the bottom. In one corner a small group of young lads and girls muttered together, they had glasses of coke and packets of crisps. By the fireplace, huddled in front of the imitation logs sat an old man, his thin, beige old man's jacket heaped on the chair beside him and a half-drunk pint of dark beer made rings on the shiny table top. What had happened to beer mats?

As Simon took in the rest of the room he felt eyes on him, he turned back, the old bloke was peering across at him. When their eyes met, the man went back to gazing at the flames but, as he reached for his drink, the glance slid sideways again.

So, presence noted and recorded. Simon leaned over and picked up his pint. It had begun.

Chapter 2

Simon rested his arms on the slightly sticky bar top, shoulders hunched, and shifted to ease the ache in his spine. The first pint slid down well and he was now half way through a second. There had been quiet movement of the few customers back and forth across the room. A couple of people had come in and found seats but nobody to cause him concern or to grab his interest. The only real life was an occasional shrill spark of laughter from the group in the corner and the buzz of the ice machine; otherwise the place remained quiet, dull. It was depressing but he couldn't yet find the will to move on. The beer was good but the event, long anticipated, had fallen short of his expectations. It was nothing new, life was disappointment and false hope, it didn't bother him much anymore. He glanced towards the clock on the wall and noted that the old bloke had slipped out, leaving an empty glass and a screwed-up scratch card as his legacy.

The afternoon moved on.

There was someone behind him now, he felt the change in temperature, the soft movement of air on his neck. He didn't turn, didn't move.

"So. You're back." Simon recognised the voice immediately, voices didn't change, faces wrinkled and muscles wasted but voices stayed the same until extreme old age. He still didn't move, not at first but then after a few heartbeats he reached out and picked up the drink, drained the contents and slapped the glass back on the bar top. The barmaid scuttered forward, cast a nervous glance over his shoulder as she took it away to the other end of the bar. He closed his eyes and heard the swish of water as she pumped it up and down on the glass cleaner.

"Not staying, are you?" He felt pressure as the man behind him leaned in even closer. More beats heavy in his chest, Simon concentrated on his breathing, holding steady. "I'm talking to you." He turned now, slowly sliding from the bar stool. Still without speaking he tipped his head a little, staring into the narrowed blue eyes only inches from his face. "I asked you a question."

Simon leaned sideways and retrieved his backpack. The pub was silent, the group in the corner stilled and the barmaid standing with her hand on the internal phone, ready to call for help.

Still he didn't speak. His right hand raised now, holding back the newcomer as he straightened and turned, pushing past. He heard the sharp intake of breath as the side of his face was revealed, the scar that snaked down from just in front of the ear to loop under his jawline.

He didn't look back, not even when he heard the new male voice, deep and serious. "You're barred Jason, I've told you before. Leave now."

Before the figure of Jason Parr – lean and muscular in jeans and a leather jacket – came through the double doors, Simon had rounded the next corner and was striding away back towards the town centre. He wasn't afraid, his heartbeat had already normalised, he wasn't ashamed of leaving without standing up before the implied threat, he just wasn't ready yet.

It was fully dark now and the wind cold and uncaring as he turned up his collar and thrust his freezing hands deep into his coat pockets. He would buy a hat tomorrow, a hat and gloves.

The traffic was thickening as the office workers and shop assistants made their thankful way home to houses that were warm and smelled of roasting meat and onions, or cats that stretched and purred and made empty spaces cosy. He dragged out the piece of paper and stopped under a street lamp to read the address again. He had an idea where the bed and breakfast was and knew also not to expect too much, not in Mill Street.

* * *

It was better than he had hoped. The area had improved and the detached house had bright windows and well-kept shrubs surrounded a tarmacked parking area. A shiny, red front door slipped open easily at his touch and warm, vanilla-scented air wrapped around him. He felt his face soften, blinked his eyes – this was nice.

"Hello love, you alright?" A slim dark-haired woman came from behind the desk pushed into a corner of the hallway. She smoothed down her narrow skirt and tucked a strand of hair behind her ear. She smiled at him. On the wall a bank of small pigeon holes held keys and there were leaflets in plastic stands beside the phone.

"Hello, I have a room booked. Fulton – Simon Fulton." She poked at the keyboard on the edge of the highly-polished surface and nodded. "Two nights?"

"For now, might be longer, will it be okay?"

"Yes, just let me know."

He nodded.

She held out a key dangling from a large wooden fob, "There's tea and coffee in the room, I don't really like you eating in there but we don't do dinner. If you're stuck you can bring something in and eat it in the dining room, just leave it tidy."

"That's pretty generous."

"Well, I try to be realistic, not everybody can afford to eat in restaurants every night. I've found it's better this way than having fish and chips and pizzas in the rooms. Gloria by the way."

"Sorry."

"My name, it's Gloria."

"Oh sorry, right – hello Gloria." Her hand was soft and warm in his, her smile genuine and her eyes sparkled as she held on just a moment longer than seemed natural. He pulled back and bent to grab his bag.

"First floor, turn right at the top of the steps; is that all your luggage?"

"What, oh yes, just this."

"Right, I thought maybe …" she waved a hand towards the door. "Maybe you left some in the car."

"No, no car. I don't have a car." She smiled again and nodded.

"Breakfast from seven to ten. I'll see you then Simon." It was taking time, getting used to the relaxed conversation, accepting what was said for just what it was, just the usual back and forth. It had been natural for him. It would be again, he just had to give it time. He had to give it all time.

The room was clean with a tiny en-suite bathroom, a chair by the window and a table holding a miniature kettle, a basket filled with sachets of coffee, tea bags, tiny cups of milk substitute and a couple of mugs.

He had eaten sandwiches on the coach and the two pints of beer had filled his belly so he had no appetite, no need to untidy the downstairs dining room. He took a long, long shower and slipped under the duvet. It took a few minutes for the bed to warm but as it did he felt the knots in his muscles untie and he closed his eyes. Now, he let himself think of Sandie, for the first time in years. As tears slid out from under his closed lids he turned his head into the pillow and let the grief have its way.

Chapter 3

"More, Simon?" Gloria stood beside the table, a tray of stainless steel pots balanced on one arm.

"Great, lovely breakfast, thanks." She nodded at him, left the teapot and moved on to deliver hot drinks to the other two occupied tables. It *had* been a good breakfast; the best food he had eaten for a long time. In the last two days there had been sandwiches, burgers and chips but none of them on a proper plate, eaten with a knife and fork. Civilised. These little things had been pushed away, not possible and thus consigned to the mental box he had constructed to hold the things of his past. It was only now as they crept back into his life that he understood how much they had meant.

He felt stuffed, he was warm and after another shower when he got out of bed he was beginning to feel clean.

Gloria walked back to the kitchen smiling at him as she passed, "Have you decided how long you want to stay Simon?"

"Not exactly but can I keep the room till the end of the week?"

"Yeah, that's fine. So, last night and then four more nights."

"Great, and then Saturday I should be able to be more specific."

"Work, is it?"

"No, personal stuff." She nodded.

"If you could let me take your card details before you go out today. I would have got them last night but you'd paid the first two nights online so ..." She shrugged her shoulders and moved off. She was nice, friendly and he hadn't expected it. Could she not tell? Not from the booking, he had been told that, it was anonymous, just an online booking, no hint of where from. An innocent address. But he'd been told that everyone would know when they met him. They said you couldn't hide it, that the stink went with you and stuck around, maybe even forever.

When he left, they had given him his clothes, his bag and some money. They had offered the address of a place he could go, an organisation to help him, but he'd had enough of that, enough of everyone knowing where he was every minute, every hour. Right now, he thought, at this moment only Gloria knew where he was and she knew nothing else. Yes, there were others in the room but he was of as little interest to them as they were to him. Actually, Jason Parr knew, as did old Jack from the pub. They knew he was back. He shook his head, why try to kid himself, by now they would all know, it would have spread like flame before the wind, they would know he was 'here somewhere', he was near. Would they worry? Maybe a couple of them would panic. He hoped so.

He went back to his room and out of habit made the bed, tidied the little space.

Now, there was time to go and buy some essentials, toothpaste, soap, shampoo. There had been tiny samples in the bathroom but he wanted to be unrestrained in the luxury of the shower, to let the scent and the soap and the heat wash it all away, as quickly as possible. He needed a new razor, aftershave. He needed some clothes.

His discharge grant was nearly gone, although the travel warrant had been enough for his bus, there had been drinks, food, it had just dissolved, what looked like a reasonable amount lasted no time at all.

So, he already had his new debit card. There was money in the account and it had all been sorted, they had made sure there would be no hiccups. They had warned him not to apply for credit, not for a long, long time.

* * *

The stroll into town was good. Stretching his legs and not being aware of the distance before him, starting from a place he didn't know well. Passing different doors, unfamiliar streets. The weather was dryer but still cold, he stopped at a street stall and bought gloves, a woollen hat. It used most of the cash he had left so at the bank he drew out fifty pounds and slid it into his pocket.

The names on the shops were different – Hollister, H & M, Next, Primark – it was bewildering, the music, the dim lighting; how could you be expected to buy clothes when you couldn't see them? It flummoxed him, which were a rip off, which were cheap tat? In the end he headed for Marks and Spencer – his mother's favourite. As he stepped through the automatic door he was hit head on by her memory, the self-important way she would move between racks, thrilled that now there were two wages coming in to the house, she could come here; that she could afford to buy a winter coat from them once every two years, that her underwear was Saint Michael and her best dress had the magic label. His mum, the only person still untainted and that only because she had been gone before any of it had happened. Gone before Sandie was fourteen, dead thank God, taken by the traitorous reproduction of faulty cells, before it had all gone to hell.

The sense of his mother followed him around, he felt her proud smile, her approval as he bought socks, underwear. Christ, when did it become so complicated to buy underpants? He chose some jeans and a couple of sweaters.

"Put your card in the machine." The woman didn't even look at him, she was packing his new clothes into a bag. He had held out the card expecting her to take it from him.

"Machine? Sorry I don't know…" She glanced up and dragged the card reader across the counter. Simon turned to watch the woman next to him slide her plastic into the slot.

"Right, right sorry, stuff on my mind." But he could tell by the look on the assistant's face that he had hesitated too long, made her curious. She had stopped what she was doing to watch him, a frown creasing her brows. He peered down and prayed that the number worked first time as he punched it in. Sandie's birthday, they had suggested something easy to remember, he had chosen one of the hardest numbers he knew. It worked. The woman smiled at him, ripped out the receipt and slid it into the carrier. He was already dismissed, the momentary glitch forgotten. It would be easier next time, everything was easier the second time, that's what they said wasn't it?

Chapter 4

He went back to the hotel, used the tiny kettle and made a cup of tea and then dressed in his new clothes. The old ones lay in a heap on the flowery carpet, perhaps there was a launderette, he would ask Gloria. Maybe if he offered to pay she would wash his old stuff for him.

The new things had cheered him, made him feel as though he fitted in better. Actually, thinking about it, he probably wouldn't bother with washing the old ones. He would bin them and buy some more of these jeans. He would get some shoes as well, new trainers, everyone was wearing them, even the old blokes. The only leather shoes he'd seen were on the feet of business types in their suits and overcoats.

His mood lifted as he planned it, doing ordinary things. Later though, as he turned to the hill and climbed towards the church, he felt the misery again. As before he had chosen the hard road, just like his visit to the house. It would be easier to avoid this part but he wouldn't, it was the next step and until he had done this he couldn't move on.

The church looked the same. Not really surprising, a building that had already stood for more than two hundred years wasn't going to change much in a couple of decades. He followed the path across the front and down the long side. Scaffolding had been erected at one end and he was surprised to see they were cleaning the exterior, the old stones underneath were pale and attractive, they looked naked, new-born. So, some things were changing after all. The graves were the same though. He glanced at the ancient ones nearer to the building, he remembered them from years ago, visits with school for harvest festivals, carol services and the few family weddings that he'd been to. Some of them were lopsided and the lettering just about worn away. So much for the idea of immortality.

He walked on, it was harder with every step but he kept going.

At the far corner of the graveyard the oak tree was bigger than he remembered but not much really. He went a little further and there it was, the simple marker. Why had they done it? It wasn't right to put the people you loved into the cold ground. Even though he'd been young, he'd felt that. Of course, he had no real sway with his father but had tried, told them not to leave his mum in the graveyard, but he'd been ignored.

The lump that had stuck in his throat made it hard to swallow but he gulped and coughed and shifted his shoulders. Straightening up, stiffening his spine.

Somebody had been caring for the plot. Maybe it was still the church people, he remembered there was some sort of arrangement but not how long it was supposed to last. There were no flowers, just an empty vase made of stone. He should have brought something, but it was too late. The gravel was weed-free and the headstone clean, the white words stood out clear against dark grey granite. The first inscription was for his mum and then underneath, there it was. Sandie, fourteen. His sister. He had never seen the stone with the later addition and grief doubled him over as he read her name. They had formalised it of course, Sandra Elaine, and he reached out a hand and traced the letters and wished he'd brought flowers. "A Beloved Daughter. Sleeping with the Angels." What a load of shit, she wasn't sleeping – she was dead, brutally, unfairly and horrifyingly dead – forever. The emotions kept catching him unawares, he needed to get a grip. For now though, let the tears flow. What the hell, it was a graveyard, you could cry in a graveyard, couldn't you?

He lowered to the tiny wall around the edge of the plot, perched on the cold stone and waited for his heart to empty and the cold hardness to come back. He knew it would, it always had.

"Hi Mum, Sandie. It's me." He muttered quietly, it didn't feel as silly as he might have imagined. He knew they weren't there, believed they weren't anywhere but this was the closest he could come to being with them and it would have to do. "So, I came back. I came back to see you, to see this. They didn't let me come before. Anyway, I thought I'd come, so," he shrugged his shoulders, "here I am. The thing's over. It was hard and cruel but I got through it, there were times when I nearly didn't make it." He raised his finger and traced the line of raised scar tissue down his face, "but that's not important now. I know what I have to do. Do you know? I suppose some people would say yes but … anyway, I know and that's what matters. If I get the chance I'll come back afterwards, but if I don't," he paused, "well it should never have happened to you Sandie, never you."

He couldn't find anything more to say. He raised the ends of his fingers to his lips and touched the cold stone quickly. Feeling a little over emotional, a little dramatic but deeply committed he pushed up from the grave, stood for a moment looking down and then turned sharply and marched back the way he had come.

As he swivelled through the lych gate he saw a slender figure hurry towards the end of the road and round into the path through the park. His first instinct was to call out, he had recognised her immediately even though it was just a fleeting glimpse, but as he raised his hand, he stayed his tongue. If she had seen him and turned away that told him all he needed to know, all he had expected and if she hadn't seen him – well that was for the best surely. She might have heard about him being in the pub. If so she would know that he would come here – well, whatever, that was something else that was over and had been for a long, long time.

The wind was in his face now and the water tracked across his cheeks but it was just the cold in his eyes, wasn't it? He relaxed, warming with the exercise and was almost at the town centre. He strolled around, being with strangers and remembering the familiar places. After a few hours he'd had enough, was anticipating a warm shower, more tea and then the little restaurant near his bed and breakfast. Maybe steak – yes, why not?

He didn't see them until they were almost on top of him. Three of them, jeans and dark jackets, black wool hats and scarves pulled up to cover their chins. He glanced around, the street was deserted except for the little group of men.

"You shouldn't have come. You're not welcome here. I told you, in the pub, I warned you not to stay."

As his fists clenched and muscles tightened the old anger surged up, this was sooner than he had planned but okay, so be it. If it was to be now, then so be it.

Chapter 5

He had known that there were CCTV cameras all around the town centres. There had been grumbling complaints, 'intrusion of privacy'. It was just whining, not much of a leap to work out what was really bothering the people he'd been sharing his life with up until recently, so he hadn't given them any credence. Now though, it wasn't possible to know whether the impending trouble had been seen remotely and the cameras had done him a favour, or whether it was just coincidence. It didn't really matter why, as the police car appeared round the corner, he felt a rush of relief. He hadn't been ready for a confrontation, having just left the graves he had been in the wrong mood, his head in the past, his reflexes dulled and his mind on other things. It wouldn't do for them to get the better of him first, to build up their confidence, make them cocky and arrogant and whittle away at his own resolve.

They nudged at each other as the car slowed. The one at the back, the short fat one turned away and stepped back into the alley.

Jason Parr leaned towards him. His voice was a hiss through the wool of his scarf, "Later, we'll be sorting you.

If you stay round here. You'd be best off leaving now. Straight away. You're not welcome." After he had delivered the mumbled threat they spun and shuffled off into the growing gloom.

The police car stopped, pulling into the opposite curb. The driver wound down his window, "Everything okay sir."

He had to resist an urge to laugh. He didn't reply but raised a hand to them and walked away. He couldn't become involved with them, not so soon, well not ever if it could be helped. He'd had enough of that to last a lifetime and more. They waited until he'd gone a few hundred yards up the road and then slowly drew away. He wondered if they would make a report, had there been enough for them to record; then again what had the camera seen? Still, if things went the way he planned, none of it would matter.

He had imagined that there would be more time than this though, time to plan and organise but it seemed he was to be forced to act quickly.

It was a surprise that feelings were still running so high. As he had made the plans, seeing it in his mind's eye over and over, he had imagined coming back and passing unnoticed until he made his move. He had supposed memories were short and in the time that had passed everything would have become a footnote. Tomorrow he would get on with it all. Tonight he would have his steak, a couple of drinks and lie in the warm in his cosy bed and then tomorrow the world would change again.

* * *

The steak was good and the half bottle of red wine soothed the edges of his nerves.

Gloria was in the hallway when he let himself back in through the door. "Hello Simon, been for a meal?"

"Yeah, The Saracen's Head, had a steak."

"Good was it?"

"Great actually."

18

"The chef there is a friend, I'll tell him you enjoyed his cooking." She smiled as she spoke and came across the oak flooring. "I was just going to have a nightcap, do you want to join me, just a quick one."

"Oh, okay. That would be nice actually, yeah." She turned and headed into the dining room. The big sideboard cupboard held an assortment of bottles: whisky, brandy, liqueurs. "What do you fancy?"

"I'll have a whisky, any sort."

"I'm working my way through these. We used to run a bar, back in the day." He tilted his head and raised his eyebrows, waiting for her to continue. "We used to do dinner, in the evening, before my hubby died."

"Oh, I'm sorry." A sad smile lifted the corners of her mouth.

"Yes, well, you just have to keep on, don't you? But I couldn't manage it on my own and I didn't have the heart to interview, take someone on. My Dave used to do the cooking, he could hold his own as well, could give The Saracen's Head a run for their money."

"Was it recent?"

"A few years now. He fell in the river. Stupid sod, they said he'd been drinking. It wasn't like him but there was an inquest and everything so…" She shrugged her shoulders. "Anyway, I held things together but just stopped doing the evening meals. She waved a hand in front of the open cupboard, "It left me with all this to finish off, this and the stuff we had stored. I'm getting through it though."

She had pulled out a bottle of brandy and a single malt and poured two hefty measures. "Come on, let's sit in the lounge, it's warmer." She handed him the heavy bottomed glass as she passed him on the way out of the room and across the hallway.

It was nice and cosy in her private living room, the furniture was modern and light and a log fire burned in the hearth. Simon couldn't tell whether it was real but he assumed not as there were no spare logs and the flames were even and regular but the effect was good and he sighed as he settled into the cream cushions of the easy chair.

"So, how long have you been out, Simon?" Her question flummoxed him and for a moment all he could do was stare at her, trying to form a response. She in turn simply waited, smiling at him and taking a small sip of her brandy and then swirling it in the oversized glass.

Chapter 6

"How did you know?"

"Don't look so upset. It's just experience, personal I'm afraid. My dad, my brother they were a couple of naughty boys." She gave a huff of a laugh. "Nothing too terrible I suppose but enough to get them locked up a few times. They had that look when they came home, the look that you have now and again."

"How do you mean? What look?"

"Oh, I don't know, a bit bewildered I suppose, nervous and out of step but trying to look confident somehow. Mind you there was the clothes as well, the M&S bags with your old stuff in them, old-fashioned stuff, thrown away. Most of my visitors don't bother making the beds and tidying their rooms either, though some do. Anyway, it'll fade with time, with my lot it didn't last long. They came back to my mum and me, back to the same house and soon slipped into the old life, unfortunately. They're gone now, Dad died a while ago and Peter, my brother Peter went off. I think he's down south and I haven't heard from him for ages. I keep hoping but, well ..." she lifted her shoulders in another shrug, he was beginning to see that it was a habit, an expression of acceptance. "Anyway, maybe he's okay, getting away from here, the sorts he was mixing with, all the low-lifes, dangerous people. Perhaps he's okay."

"Yeah, I hope so."

"But you, you haven't anyone to go back to?"

He shook his head in response.

"Shame, I'm sure it helps. Are you not from around here then?"

He lifted the glass, threw back his whisky and placed it carefully on the little coffee table. As he unfolded from his seat on the soft chair he looked her straight in the eye. "I'm off to bed now Gloria, thanks for the drink."

She understood that there was to be no unburdening in the quiet room and as he turned to the door she gazed into the fake flames.

* * *

The earlier confrontation in the street played and re-played in his mind. Now, with hindsight he was regretting the arrival of the police car, it meant a delay of the inevitable. If he had acted, re-acted quickly, it would all be over one way or the other instead of buzzing in his brain.

When sleep did come, it came with horrors. Waiting for Sandie delayed at a sports meeting, irritated and impatient. The cigarette butts one after the other collecting around his feet. Then afterwards, the crowds of people in the warm summer night, streets not quite dark, all of them searching. Pointless and fruitless. Then strangers with solemn faces and brutal news of a body, despoiled and abandoned in the copse by the river.

Sandie.

He tossed and turned and paced in the little room. His body was tired but he knew from bitter experience where the dream would take him if he slid back under the covers. It would consume his sleeping self. The panic and fear when he had been accused and dragged through the legal system and then the despair when they told the world that

22

it was him. He had been the one who had brutalised and murdered his sister.

So, he paced and fretted and waited for the sky to lighten and the early rain to patter against the windows and then took another shower, dressed and left the quiet house.

He would make a start, it was too soon with still a lot of the groundwork needed, but the action would make him feel better. He didn't know what time the shops opened and he was surprised to see the car park at the local DIY store already busy. Plumbers' vans, builders' flat-backed trucks and the occasional four by four filled the spaces and he pushed through the door to join the men in overalls and paint spattered jeans and sweatshirts browsing the aisles. Although he knew what he wanted it was bewildering. On the one hand this huge place suited his needs, kept him anonymous and forgettable, on the other hand there was just so much stuff.

He prowled up and down the racks; an older man in uniform came over. "Can I help you, sir?"

"What? Oh no, it's fine, I'm okay – thanks though." The assistant didn't need much to turn him away, it was early in the morning and he was probably looking forward to his bacon sandwich and tea from the takeaway van outside.

Eventually he had it all. There was a self-service till but he didn't risk it. The last thing he wanted was to draw attention to the fact that he didn't know how all this technology worked, so he queued and paid and walked back into the slightly brighter morning with the shopping bumping against his thigh. He was amused that he'd saved quite a lot, the drill had been on special offer and the fixings came in a bumper pack. The other tools had been easy to find. He had run through his cash again though and needed to get back to the bank.

He peered into the thin plastic bags, he was fired up now with morbid excitement.

Chapter 7

When he was a kid there had been a row of lock up garages at the top of the hill. The line of concrete boxes with felt roofs and big timber doors had been used by bike and car enthusiasts with no garages or by market traders with no options. He had woven his plan around them. He had known they would be perfect, isolated and in the case of the one belonging to his family only ever used by himself.

Simon was stumped to see four little bungalows behind low, stone walls. Tidy lawns and narrow driveways led out directly onto the pavement alongside the dual carriageway. He had seen it so clearly in his memory that for a short while his brain refused to accept the visual evidence and he walked back and forth peering at the small homes, wondering if indeed the garages were hidden behind them or even if perhaps he had come to the wrong place. The big old barn a few hundred yards away and the nearby road junction were proof that he had not. They were gone and the plan would have to be re-thought, right from the very start.

Back in the town centre, shops were busy and he spent a couple of hours buying more clothes. He laced up his new trainers and left the box containing his hard leather shoes in a skip. His bank account was surprisingly healthy. He hadn't had much when Sandie died but his granddad had never changed his will and so he had received his inheritance. It had been there a long time and interest from before the financial crisis had taken it up step by step until there might even be enough to last until the end. It was ironic that life had always been a struggle, payday to payday and cutting back to save for holidays and now there was more than he had ever had in his life. He had no illusions, he was not rich, but it could be enough, it wouldn't be for long after all.

He bought the local paper and scoured the adverts for storage units or garages. It seemed that nowadays if you had too much to fit in your house you took it to a facility where there was heating and security and terms and conditions, so that was no good. As he passed what used to be a shop selling bespoke corsetry he glanced sideways. As kids, they had giggled at the reinforced pink underwear displayed in the window and the memory made him smile for a moment. Now though, it was an estate agents and an idea sneaked in and began to form. He dragged the collar of his old jacket up around his chin and pulled the woollen hat lower towards his eyes and then studied the images of rental properties.

There were some little houses, some converted places offering one and two bedroom flats and then in another window a small display of shops and a workshop. They were down at heel and tatty, out of the town centre in forgotten districts where people passed through and only stopped if they were desperate for cigarettes or a can of drink. Dross, perfect dross.

He swung away from the old shop front and crossed the road. In the warm of The Old Oak he ordered fish and chips and a pint. As he waited for the food to arrive, he began to re-organise his plan – it would have to be done differently but there were definitely possibilities.

He bought a sandwich and a bottle of blended scotch, he wouldn't use the boarding house dining room later but the snack would keep him going until morning. He needed to get back, turn on the television and let his mind wander. He knew from past experience that it was the best way for him to plan, to let his subconscious have its way and to wait for the scheme to fall into place.

Gloria was busy at her computer when he let himself back into the Bed and Breakfast. "Can I stay for another week Gloria – is that okay?"

"Yes, of course. That'll take us until next Saturday – yeah."

"Great."

"Do you want a drink, a cup of tea?" He was going to refuse but she appeared really keen and it didn't need to take long.

"Lovely, that's very kind. Thanks."

She brought out cake and fussed a bit with plates and napkins but he just let it all flow over him. The normality and the niceness of it. He could see his mum when she was trying to impress the neighbours, giving the cups an extra polish in the kitchen and making sure the spoons matched. It was from before and it choked him a little. "Are you so kind to all your tenants?"

She blushed and bent to pour the tea, hiding her heightened colour.

"Well, you seem to be on your own and I just thought you'd like the company. I didn't mean to pressure you or anything."

"No, oh God no, you didn't. It's just really nice of you."

"Well, the evening can drag a bit."

"Don't you get out much then?"

She shook her head. "It's my own fault, I should have made more effort, I do know that but to be honest there's

26

nowhere I want to go. The town's a bit dead and I'm not a 'joiner in'. We were a unit me and my hubby, busy with this place you know and enough for each other." Her eyes had brimmed and Simon squirmed, he couldn't cope with tears.

"Sorry, sorry Simon, it's just been a long day and…" she wagged a hand in the air, "I'm being a bit silly. Here, take your tea, do you want cake?"

"Thanks." He stayed with her for an hour, drank her tea and ate her Victoria sponge and began to see how she could help him. He would let it stew, try to give his brain room for the ideas to form. Many empty hours had taught him that if you just let it run, plans could make themselves. The difference this time was that, at last, the plans would have purpose.

Chapter 8

The little terraced house in Faith Street was haunting him. If he went back though he would very possibly be seen, but it was the only way he might see his father. All the time he'd been away he had waited; every visitor's day he had hoped. As the endless, dreary, wasted days and years had fallen into the abyss of time he had eventually understood that the look on his father's face, as he had been taken from the court room, might well be the last memory he had of the man who had raised him.

He had turned and peered up into the gallery, searched the faces and there he had been, eyes flat and empty and his mouth turned down in disgust. Simon had sent out a silent plea, '*Believe in me – please, if you believe me then I can cope.*' But if the old man had seen he hadn't understood. Grief, still red and raw over the loss of Sandie had left him with no room for any other emotion. No room for pity, but Simon had hoped that there might have been room for belief, or at the least for doubt.

He would know by now that Simon was back, so should he go, try to explain; try at the very least to find if there was any chance of reconnection? He sighed. What would be the point when it would be so short lived and end with yet more heartbreak? No, he would keep away, leave that part in the past.

He let himself go into the quiet and the darkness and made his mind a blank save for one thought. Revenge. It worked as he had known it would. By the time he rolled over and pulled the duvet up to his chin, the bare bones of a new plan were there.

The next morning, he ate breakfast, he smiled and chatted with Gloria and pushed away the sneaking guilt. He would use her yes, but he wouldn't hurt her and at the end of the day the task at hand was all that mattered. He stopped short of calling her collateral damage but a nub of shame joined the other negative feelings tucked away and ignored except in the unguarded moments when he allowed himself to be as he used to be. Decent, honest and good.

He spent the morning walking around the town, rediscovering more old haunts. The school was still going, he heard the yell and laughter of the children from a long way off and was drawn to the railings, to stand and watch the swirl of colour and the rush and dash of young bodies in the playground.

The printer's office where he had worked for just over five years had closed. The old signage was long gone and, on the bare wooden frontage there was no indication of whether the firm had moved to a better address or just dissolved and disappeared. White paint had been daubed on the insides of the windows and it was obvious the property itself was empty. He noted the number of the agency, scribbled it down on the edge of a bag that had held his sandwich. This was it, wasn't it? This was the right place.

The day was bright and surprisingly warm so he followed the roads upwards and then turned from the tarmac onto a dirt path, over the stile and out onto the moor. It was blowy and wild with streaks of white cloud striating the blue and he lay down on the top of a huge flat boulder. He watched the world move on and listened to the wind and wished things were better, that Sandie was still alive and that he was still a printer's apprentice, frustrated and angry in this boring little place.

Now that he had come back, the lack of his sister was a constant ache. Back when it happened, worry and panic had filled the place that should have held his grief and afterwards the only way to survive had been to build a mental wall, thick and impervious with all the horror held behind it. Now, under the open sky, he was overwhelmed with the reality of loss and the helpless fury of longing.

When the light began to dull and fade, he took the path over the tops, down into town past the mill, converted into flats while he was away, and then through to The Oak again for some food and a couple of pints. He didn't see anyone he knew but that didn't necessarily mean that he hadn't been seen, Jason Parr wasn't one to leave things to chance.

It was after seven when he made his way back to Mill Lodge and the warmth of Gloria's welcome. He hung about outside until he saw her little living room light come on and then rang the doorbell.

"Sorry Gloria, I left my key in my other jeans."

"Oh, that's okay. Come on in, have you had a good day?"

"Been out on the moor for a walk, it was lovely. Do you go up there yourself?"

She lowered her head, shook it slowly. "No, not any more. Another of those things that I let go. We used to love it. I tried it a couple of times but on my own, you know – it just wasn't the same and it was too hard."

"I enjoyed it today, maybe if you felt like it…" he left the invitation unfinished and she didn't respond. As she turned away, she spoke, "I was just going to have a drink, if you fancy one." She didn't wait but paused for a moment at the door to her private rooms. With a nod, he caught up and stepped in, holding the door for her as she went in before him and brought glasses and a bottle of Jura to where he had settled onto the settee. She held it up for him to see and as he nodded approval she poured the drinks and smiled at him, handing the whisky across the low table.

Chapter 9

They settled before the steady flames and she told him more about her husband, the chef. She surprised him with recollections of hiding boxes of cigarettes bought from the back of lorries, crates of booze from people he met at the pub. So, it hadn't only been her brother and her dad who had mixed in questionable company. He didn't detect disapproval or any hint of bravado at skirting the edges of lawlessness, just acceptance of the way things were, an odd sort of innocence.

"Were you away for long?" She used the same terminology as himself when referring to his incarceration. He shrugged and lifted the glass to his mouth and so she left it. He knew that for her the time in jail was part of him, probably the most important part– up to now – and as she was dipping her toes into the shallows of friendship she wanted to know all of it. He steered the conversation away.

"You've no kids then, Gloria?"

"No, never wanted any to be honest. Couldn't be doing with all that work and commitment. We were enjoying ourselves too much and trying to get ahead, with this place." She glanced around at the walls of her living room. "We were doing well. We had a mortgage of course but Dave reckoned we could increase it. He handled that side of things but we were hoping to buy the hotel next door, expand. We thought we might do a sort of wedding venue thing, there's a nice garden – views over the moors," she sighed, "we had plans."

"It's a shame. You know, that you didn't get the chance."

"Yeah well, story of my life really. Every time things start to get going something comes in to screw it up. Still, I never imagined that I'd lose him – not like that."

They talked until just before midnight. As they stood and she gathered up the glasses and bottles he bent and kissed her cheek lightly. She coloured and lowered her face.

"Nice evening, Gloria, thanks so much. I'd forgotten what it could be like. Thanks." And he left her in the middle of her neat, bright room.

The next morning, he was the only guest and Gloria came to sit with him in the breakfast room and share a pot of tea. "What are you up to today then?"

"It's fine out – I thought I might go for another walk on the moors. Give myself a last day off and then tomorrow I'll need to start to sort things a bit, see about what comes next. I'm really comfortable here Gloria, it's great but I do need to decide what to do. You know, I should make up my mind whether to stay, move on – all that stuff."

She didn't answer but nodded her head and then turned to look out of the window. "Well I have rooms available, this time of the year there aren't many walkers or climbers so you don't have to rush. If you like we could even come to some sort of arrangement with the price – for a longer term booking. You can give yourself some time, adjust. She stopped short of suggesting that he stay but the hint was there."

"That's really great, really kind, but I think I need to do something more concrete. I have to decide about work, a proper home, a place of my own. I'm happy here but..." he paused until the silence grew and she was forced to fill it.

"Well, I suppose I know what you mean. At least it should be easy enough to find somewhere round here I think – not that there's much to keep you – ha. Well, if I can do anything to help just let me know." He laid a hand over hers.

"I was so lucky to come and stay here, you're lovely, d'ya know that. Honestly, I was a bit scared, didn't know what to expect and it could have been so different. I wouldn't have known how to manage, straight away – on my own. Even now the shops scare me a bit, I haven't even tried the supermarket yet."

He grinned at her but she knew that it was all true, and the fact that he was having trouble adjusting told her much of what she needed to know.

"You've been so helpful and, oh what's the word – accepting – yeah, accepting."

Again, her face flushed and she stood, apparently flustered by his words and began to gather up the dirty plates and dishes.

"Well, you know – I probably understand a bit better than some, how things can go the wrong way and how tricky it can be afterwards. As I say, if I can help you just ask."

"Maybe you'd like to come out with me today, up on the hills."

Almost before he had finished speaking she was shaking her head.

"No, I don't think so, thanks. I have stuff to do, new guests coming later on, and then the accounts. I hate them. I was never any good at that stuff. So anyway, sorry but no, not today thanks."

He should slow down a bit, stop pushing so hard. He had to let her come closer. "Right, of course. Well I think I'll go up and walk as far as The Red Lion, have a bite of lunch."

"Oh yes, they do a lovely roast."

"It's changed then. They used to do a hot pasty but that was all as far as I remember."

"That was years ago, it's much better now." As she spoke he knew that the information would seep in. She was sharp, already from the things he had let her know, she would know he was local but that he had been locked up for a fair while.

They had suggested, pre-release, that he change his name. His first reaction had been to refuse but now he saw the sense in it. If he had come to the door as Tommy Webb she probably wouldn't be quite so kind, so ready to be his friend. Even with her dodgy family background his was one name that would have caused her to back off.

Chapter 10

He went back to stand outside the empty printer's office, there were rooms above. It would do. Of course he could just take it, break in and use it but he needed time. Time to prepare and then time let it run through to the end, on his own terms. No, he had to have it for himself, for as long as it took. He had to keep his head down though, not draw attention to his activities. The last thing he wanted now was people researching his background for any reason. He needed help and had already decided where he would turn. She had warmed to him already.

The day passed as the others had, prowling the shops until he was tired and cold and then sitting in the manufactured cosiness of yet another pub. It surprised him that he hadn't met more people he knew. Now and again there had been a figure he recognised and he had turned away, slipped inside whatever shop was handy. The old crowd couldn't have all left though surely, then again there was a noticeable change in the mix of people walking around. There were more foreigners, more women with headscarves, men in baggy trousers and there were too many youngsters trailing around aimlessly. Too much unemployment, too much hopelessness. It was obvious this part of Yorkshire still struggled, it was just that the victim mix had changed.

He was supposed to have signed on by now, filled in forms and registered for work but that wasn't happening, not now – probably not ever. As long as his money lasted he would keep contact with the authorities as little as humanly possible.

He bought some snacks to store in his room, crisps and crackers, some biscuits, cheese. He shopped in a small supermarket for cans of lager and a half bottle of whisky.

The weather was dull and cold with spiteful rain blowing in the chilly wind. He wouldn't go to the moors today but he stayed out as long as he could. Walking freely up and down the roads, through the parks and then calling in for cups of coffee, another pint. Such ordinary things, such special things. He pushed away the temptation to visit the north side of town, the church, his dad's house. It would be best not to go there, not yet. Maybe later, just one more time before the end.

He knew that Gloria's mornings were her busiest time. With a young woman from nearby for help, she cleaned the rooms that had been used overnight, including his own. She cleared up after the breakfast service and did a general tidy up in her little kingdom. So, he left it until late afternoon, picked up a sandwich cake at a confectioner's shop and went back to Mill Lodge.

He let himself in and, as she wasn't in the dining room or sitting at the computer in the tiny reception area, he knocked on the door to her own rooms.

"Oh, hello Simon, come in." She was dressed casually in soft trousers and a sweat top, her dark hair was pulled up into a messy knot on the top of her head. She looked young and pretty.

"I don't want to disturb you."

"No, you're not, not at all. I was just slobbing about to be honest. I don't have any guests coming until later so I thought I'd have a bit of down time. It's always a risk, if someone knocks on the door looking for digs I don't like to look scruffy but this time of the year I sometimes get away with it."

"Oh, sorry. I'll leave you to it."

"No, don't be daft. Come on, come in – I'll put the kettle on." He held out the white box tied with ribbon.

"I brought this, a bit of a thank you for the hospitality."

"It's what you're paying me for."

"Well, yes but not the evenings, not the drinks."

She shrugged and grinned at him. "I enjoyed that as well. So, are you planning on standing there much longer?" She moved into her room and left him to follow and close the door as he handed over the cake.

"Oh lovely. That's a gorgeous little confectioner. I'm so glad we still have one or two independent shops. It's the walkers that keep them going really, people on holiday like a bit of local colour don't they. Of course, most people go to the retail park now. It's a shame. Anyway, enough of that I'll get some plates. Tea or coffee?"

"Coffee would be great, if you're sure I'm not disturbing you."

"Oh, would you stop? I've told you." As she laughed and walked through to her little kitchen he sat down on the cream sofa. He should have taken his shoes off and was horrified to see that he had trailed mud onto the carpet.

"Shit."

"What's the matter?"

"Sorry, sorry Gloria, 'scuse me. I've made a mess on the floor here, with my shoes."

"Oh never mind, here. She tossed a cloth to him. "Give it a rub with that, will that work?"

"Yeah, great – sorry about that." He rubbed the stain on the carpet and then gathered the damp rag and carried it to the kitchen door. She was just inside, pouring water into the cafetiere and he tried to push past to drop the cloth into the sink. As he brushed behind her he felt the slightest of touches, his hip against hers, it was little more than a disturbance of the air between them but he felt her tense. He tossed the cloth into the sink and backed away clumsily; he almost fell back onto the settee. The silence was charged until she picked up the tray and spoke just a little more loudly than was normal.

"It's a lovely cake, lemon sandwich. Haven't had one of these for ages," she said.

"Good, I hoped you'd like it. That shop, it was full of stuff I didn't recognise, carrot cake, God I wonder what my mum would have made of that, and brownies – what the heck are brownies? I thought they were little Girl Guides."

She started to giggle now and it was all okay again. As she licked a smear of filling from her fingers she looked across at him. "A bit odd this really."

"What is, what's odd?"

"Well, don't get offended, will you?"

"No, no, I won't."

"Well this, it's a bit – oh I don't know, genteel I suppose is the only word I can think of."

"Genteel."

"Yes, you bringing a sandwich cake."

"Oh, should I not have done it?"

"No, no it's not that – it's just that – well, knowing where you've been, how life must have been for you…"

"Ah right, yeah. I'll be honest it did feel odd. Standing in the queue in the shop with all those women, buying teacakes and scones but you know while I was away, in all that – oh if I call it basic-ness, do you know what I mean?"

She nodded.

"Well my mum and the things she used to do, the stuff we used to have, it was what I tried to focus on. It's hard, almost impossible not to be brutalised by it, to become something that I didn't want to become and I tried to fight it. I put all this stuff, the 'nice' stuff into a place in my mind and tried to keep it clean, you know, make it not part of what I was living," Simon continued

"Well I have to say you've done a pretty good job. I wouldn't have known. Looking at you today I wouldn't guess," Gloria replied.

He grinned over at her. "Really, do you really mean that?"

"Yeah, I really do."

"That's just about the best thing you could have said to me."

"It was just the once, wasn't it?"

He drew in a breath, he hadn't intended to talk about it but now here it was, no way out without being rude, upsetting her. "Yes. Just once."

"I thought so, you don't seem the sort like my dad, my brother. In and out over and over until that life was as normal to them as this one. Look, I don't want to pry, I won't but if you want to talk about it, anytime – well, I'm here."

He didn't answer her, just nodded his head once. He stood and bent to put his plate onto the tray.

"It's okay, leave them. I need to get a move on anyway. I have to get changed and go and double check the guest rooms." She glanced at the tiny gold watch on her wrist. "Bloody hell yes, they'll be here soon. Thanks for the cake Simon."

He waved a hand at her and stepped to the door. "Thanks for the company – again – Gloria. See you later, yeah."

"Yes, see you later, come down for a drink maybe. About eightish."

Chapter 11

A skeleton of the plan had been with him for years. He had to go slowly, had to hold on; to rush it could mean failure. Then again, maybe he should change it all, just go in like a tempest, and afterwards find his own peace. He could, he knew he could. All this planning and waiting and cleverness wasn't necessary, it was stage business and self-indulgence.

He stood before the window trying to find calm, looking out at the hills, it worked, always had. The claustrophobia when they had first locked him up had been vile. Gooseflesh popped on his arms as he remembered the nights when he lay, sweating and panicked in the tiny cell. The ceiling pressing down and the walls squeezing the breath from him until he had to leap up and pace back and forth, counting steps, the screams held at bay only by the knowledge that if they could say he was mad then there was a chance that he would never be released. He had wanted to pound the door, kick his way through and run and run back to the moors. Of course the moors weren't there, no matter how long he might have run and however fast, and the door was impenetrable. So, he learned to deal with it, to work out in the gym until he was exhausted and the panic was held back and fed into the hate. It had left him physically strong, he was tougher than he looked. He was convinced that if he wanted to, he could do it all now, take them all on and win. But he needed more than victory, he needed revenge therefore he must go slowly.

His nerves began to settle. The short grass rippling in the breeze and the gleam of moisture on the dark leaves of gnarly shrubs was timeless, it helped.

There was a decent sized garden here. A couple of groups of metal tables and spindly looking chairs furnished a flagged patio and over towards the low, dry stone wall a wooden bench gazed out to the hills. He could see how it would make a lovely setting in the summer, a marquee on the huge lawn and wedding photographs taken with the endless sky and the rolling roughness of moorland as a backdrop. He imagined that Gloria and her husband had been right about the potential and her frustration at the aborted scheme could well be a tool he could use. He turned away to sit on the small bedroom chair. That sort of stuff, weddings and parties, frivolity, was part of another world, Sandie's world really and his mum's, not his though. Not now and not ever.

The next day was overcast and chilly but he couldn't stay in the room, he needed to move, to breathe fresh air and feel the wind in his face. There were several pubs doing food and he spent a few hours at the corner table in The Oak.

On the way back to the hotel he picked up a pizza, it would be cold by the time he ate it but that was fine. It was a quiet day but for him not empty. It was filled with freedom and when he slid into bed and turned on the tiny television he was as content as was reasonable, for a while he had let the tangles in his brain rest and refused to let the future taint the present; it wasn't honest, he knew that, but none of this was and he had accepted that, for now at least. He let it be.

* * *

"Did you sleep well Simon?" He was late into breakfast and Gloria paused on her way back to the kitchen with a tray of dirty dishes.

"Yeah, great thanks."

"So, today? What have you got planned?" He shook his head and lowered his gaze to the empty plate.

"I'm supposed to go and sign on."

"Ah yes. Do you know where the office is?"

"Yes, I saw it the other day but," he stopped, tightened his lips.

"What, what's the matter?"

"I've never done it. Before, I worked. I always worked, right from leaving school. It just feels bad. I don't really want to do it."

"But you won't be able to claim your benefit if you don't."

"I know, but I just keep imagining my mum, what she would say. She was always so proud of the fact that I went straight into work. It feels as though I'm letting her down – ha, that's a laugh, as if I haven't done that already."

"Is she still alive – your mum?"

"No, she's not. She died a while ago, thank God before my troubles. Sorry Gloria, this isn't your problem. It's just getting me down a bit – the thought of it."

"Well, I guess you don't have many options do you?"

He didn't answer her, this was too easy. *Steady, steady take it slowly.*

"Well, you know while I was away, I studied. I did computer stuff and art and I kind of had an idea."

"Oh right," she had put the tray down and lowered to the chair opposite to him. "What was that then, your idea?"

"I thought maybe I could have my own business. It's daft of course, I do know that, it was just a silly dream really."

Well, you should keep hold of your dreams Simon. We had ours, plans and schemes you know, ours didn't work out but maybe yours could."

I just thought that I could do advertising stuff, printing posters, banners."

"But can't people do that themselves? Everyone has a computer now."

"Yeah, of course. Little flyers and things like that but I was thinking of the big stuff, those big plastic flags that you see at festivals and banners for businesses."

"Oh well, I suppose somebody does those. I'd never thought about it. But round here there wouldn't be much call for it, I don't think."

"No, probably not, but it doesn't matter, does it? Not these days. You can do it all on the internet. People prefer it I think, well that's what they told us anyway. All you need are some premises tucked away, it could be anything – a garage, a house, a little shop. You don't need big flash showrooms. As I say I did some courses and it's all there online."

He had to be careful, this must look new. There must be nothing to connect him with Tommy Webb – not even a past in the printing trade but he knew that he would be able to talk about it knowledgably if necessary and it was true about the extra training. Anything to pass the time and keep his brain alive, to fill the useless days. Course after course, anything that was available.

"Oh well, there we are then. I hadn't really thought about it but you're probably right. It makes sense doesn't it, you can be based anywhere I suppose."

"That's it – I thought maybe I could have a go but – well no it's stupid. I couldn't do that not right now, not with my history."

"It's a shame. I know just what it feels like to have your plans and not be able to get on with them."

"Yeah well, anyway I think I'll hold off for a bit, with the signing on you know. I can manage for a while."

She reached over and squeezed his arm. "It's going to be hard, Simon, to get on. It really is."

He nodded at her and conjured up a smile. "Ah well, I can dream, can't I? It's frustrating though, I'm sure I could make it work and I have some money, and I think there might be enough to get me started but – well, nobody is going to help me, are they?"

"No, I'm afraid not. Not if you're honest with them, and I think you have to be, don't you? You can't start off on the wrong foot, it'll come back to bite you in the future if you do. Are there no organisations that are, you know, specific for your situation?"

"Probably. I don't want to do that though, I want to start completely new, leave it behind, do you know what I mean? Ah well." He pushed his chair back and turned away from the table. "I'll just go and have a walk anyway, go up on the tops, it always makes me feel better."

"You should have some better clothes, going up on the hills at this time of the year. You should have a good waterproof jacket, some boots. What size do you take?"

"Yes, you're probably right, I could go to the big shop in town, the cut price place, see what they've got."

"Tell you what, I still have some of my hubby's stuff. If they'll fit you then I'd be more than happy to let you use them."

"No, no I couldn't – God, that's so kind of you but – well I don't know. Are you sure?"

"Yes, it's silly having them in the cupboard and you out there in that thin jacket, your trainers."

As he turned onto the dirt path, dressed in a good quality waterproof jacket and his feet in leather hiking boots, Simon allowed a smile to play around his mouth. He had her, he knew he had her.

Chapter 12

"What do you want me to do with the boots and stuff, Gloria?"

"Keep them for now if you like, use them. Did you have a good walk?"

"Yeah, I did, it's always beautiful up there."

"Good, you're looking better, got some colour in your cheeks these days." She smiled at him, reached a hand forward and then drew it back and folded her arms tight across the front of her body. "So, what now?"

"I'm going into town for a bit, got some stuff to do. Perhaps see you later?"

"I'm out tonight so if you'll be late make sure you take your key," Gloria replied.

"Oh right. Well, have a good time."

She smiled and nodded at him as she turned away, if she had caught the flash of disappointment on his face she didn't react.

He had a shower and went into town to the library where he knew there was a computer suite. It wasn't dissimilar to the one he had used while he'd been in jail, but smaller and obviously with a greater mix of users. He was directed to a vacant desk and settled down placing the scrap of paper beside the keyboard. The librarian came to stand behind him as he logged on, Simon paused and turned, "Yes?"

"Do you need any help sir, logging on or whatever?"

"No, it's fine thanks. I'm okay, my own system has gone down and I just have some stuff I need to do. I can print stuff out here, yeah?"

"Certainly, there is a small charge per copy."

"Yeah, fine – great."

He found the site of the agents dealing with the little shop. The lease was more than he had expected but well within his budget. He printed out the details. It was very scruffy but he wasn't bothered about that and it probably meant that they would ask fewer questions, just be glad to get it off their hands.

* * *

He was used to sleepless nights; they didn't bother him anymore. They were preferable to the tormented dreams that followed him even now after all this time. When the hours crawled by and his mind refused to shut down he let it run, let it plan and enjoyed the feeling of being alone, in a warm cocoon, free and his own man again. He ran over the ideas, made a mental list of the things that he would still need, the way he would finesse it all and by the time the birds began to stir and the little gaps around his curtains brightened he was buzzing with the need to get it going.

He tidied up and went down to the dining room. "Morning Gloria, did you have a nice evening?"

"It was okay, nothing special but I have to make the effort now and again."

"Oh, right. Maybe one evening we could do something – sorry that was forward of me, sorry." She blushed and lowered her eyes, busy straightening the table setting.

"That would be nice Simon, I'd like that – yeah."

47

"Oh, great smashing. So, what shall we do? A meal, would you come with me to The Saracens Head, it's nice in there, isn't it?"

"Great, that would be lovely but could we do somewhere else?"

He remembered that she knew the people who worked in the place he had suggested. He understood but was still offended that she didn't want to be seen with him. He beat it back. It didn't matter. "Okay, tell you what you decide. Tonight then?"

"Oh, erm – okay then, why not? I'll look forward to it. I'll ring that new place up by the old cinema, book us a table. It's Italian I think – is that okay?"

"Smashing, yeah that'd be great." She grinned at him and turned to carry the dirty plates back to the kitchen. As she went through the swing door she glanced back over her shoulder and gave him another beaming smile.

He went back to his bedroom for his backpack. He dropped the print out from the library on the floor outside his bedroom door.

He was struggling to rid himself of the irritation he felt at breakfast until he realised that Gloria's reluctance to be seen in his company could have nothing to do with who he was – she didn't know. So, it was just reluctance to be seen with a man, any man. He grinned, okay, yes that's okay.

Chapter 13

The restaurant was warm and welcoming and there were enough customers to create a lively atmosphere.

Simon had been to M&S during the afternoon and bought a new sweater and a pair of trousers. He realised that he needn't have bothered, many of the men, and the women for that matter were wearing jeans and sweatshirts. Obviously the idea of dressing up for a night out was outdated. On the other hand, it made the occasion special for him, and there had been none of those in his recent past. He noticed that Gloria had dressed up and wore more makeup than usual. He told her how pretty she looked, the compliment came easily to his lips.

They ordered, pasta and chicken dishes, salad, garlic bread and a bottle of wine. He had let her take the lead and was grateful that she understood without anything being said that he was a bit out of his depth.

"Have you been here before, Gloria?"

"No, but I wanted to, it's lovely isn't it."

"Yes, this is the first time I've been anywhere like this. Before…" he waved a hand, "you know – I used to go to that place on the high street, I noticed it's gone now, it was

Indian." He had spoken without thinking and realised that he had given away more of his past than intended. She didn't comment on the revelation, instead she laughed.

"What, what's funny?"

"Oh, it's nothing, well I don't know if it's true but they closed down because someone said that dead cats had been found in the freezer, skinned and ready to cook." She raised a hand to her mouth and her eyes grew round with amusement and mock horror.

"Shit – you're kidding."

She shook her head, giggling now. "It's probably not true. Anyway, it finished them, nobody would go there after that was in the papers."

"Yeah, well people are really influenced by that stuff, aren't they? You know, it's in the papers so it must be true." Illogically under the circumstances he had to work to hold back the anger that spurted up from the dark place where he kept his hate.

"Well anyway, this is nicer, isn't it?"

"Yeah, that's one thing I noticed, there are a lot more eating places now. Back in the day there was just the Indian and the fish and chip shops." If she could be bothered she could now work out when he had last lived here but it seemed that being more open with her was bringing her closer, and so it was worth the risk.

"Yeah, well again it's down to the tourists. It's saved this place really. That silly television programme started it, you know the one about those old blokes and the woman with the wrinkled stockings. It made people take notice and then the coach trips started coming up here and we all benefitted."

"But that wasn't here, was it?" Simon asked.

"No but it's not that far away and we have the waterfall and the glen. The steep streets, stone houses – all of that stuff is apparently quaint and charming now." She gave a laugh. "My gran used to curse the hills when her arthritis was bad! It's a funny world. Mind you I'm not knocking it, we did okay out of it, me and Dave."

The food arrived and for a while they ate in silence and when it began to stretch into awkwardness Gloria was the one to fill it. She put down her cutlery and reached into the bag she had hung on the back of her chair.

"Is this yours Simon?" It was the printed page showing the picture of the tatty shop.

"Oh, yeah." Simon tipped his head to one side and frowned. "I thought it was in my room."

"Oh, right well, it was on the landing on the floor."

"Sorry."

"No, no, it's okay, I guessed it must be yours. I'll put it back in my bag, remind me when we get back."

"Thanks Gloria." He waited for her to ask him about it but her comments were about the chicken, the music, the splattering of rain that blew against the window.

Eventually he took charge, "I spotted that place when I was out walking the other day," he pointed to her bag. "It's a grotty little shop up behind the old Chapel."

"Oh right."

She was maddeningly incurious.

"It has a flat, upstairs."

"Yeah I had a little look at the details. It's not that nice though, is it?"

"Well no, but it's cheap and the lease allows for internal alterations."

"Is this to do with your idea, your advertising thing?"

"Yeah," he laughed quietly, "I can't help thinking about it, planning it. It's stupid, isn't it?"

"No, no, don't say that."

"Well, it's not going anywhere. I mean nobody is going to let me rent, all that sort of thing, not with my history."

"Hmm, I suppose not. Have you asked?"

He shook his head. "No real point, they would want references and so on…"

"But isn't there any way you could get those? I mean," she stopped and he saw her visibly screw up her courage. "Look, I said I wouldn't ask you about it and I won't but if whatever the trouble was, it wasn't to do with – oh, I don't know fraud, business stuff – then surely you could get some references from somewhere."

Before she had finished speaking he was shaking his head. "I am really grateful for the way you've been about it all, Gloria, but honestly, I know I wouldn't be able to get references. I'm not in touch with anyone since before, I cut off all connections, there's nobody, I don't want to be in touch with anybody from back then. Oh, don't worry about it, it's just my daft idea and it's not going anywhere. Come on, let's order our puddings and forget all that stuff."

He watched, knew the ideas whirled in her mind and the feeling of success was only slightly marred by a smaller one of guilt.

Chapter 14

"Do you want to come in for a nightcap?"

"Yeah, that'd be nice. It's been a lovely evening, Gloria, thanks so much. It was special. Can I just say thanks, thanks for the way you've been?" He raised a hand and covered his eyes for a moment.

"Oh come on, you daft thing – don't go getting all soppy on me."

"Sorry. You've no idea though, really. I was away for a long time, Gloria, a long time and I was scared shitless about coming out – excuse my French – but I was, and you've been so lovely."

"Yeah well, I told you, I can understand better than some people."

"Did they know, when they made the booking for me – did they know that you'd had dealings with, oh, what shall I call it, the law?"

"God no, I couldn't let anyone know about that stuff. I'd be out of business in no time. I suppose you've gathered by now that I'm not actually from here. I was born in Leeds, moved here when Dave and I got married. It felt good to get away, make a new start."

"Right, well it all just seems too good to be true to be honest."

"No – just chance. So, whisky is it?"

"Lovely." She brought the drinks and lit the fire and came to curl in the chair beside the settee with her legs drawn up under her. It was calm and quiet and for a moment he wished that he could let it all go and that this could be real, but this was not his. This was what other people had.

She leaned over the arm of the chair and pulled her bag up from the floor where she had dropped it as they walked into the room. She held out the printed paper. "There you go."

"Oh thanks." He screwed the paper into a small ball and threw it into the waste bin.

"What did you do that for?"

"Because it was nonsense. I can't do any of this stuff, I have to just go and sign on and then see if I can find a job somewhere. Mind you, I don't think there'll be anything round here, will there? I don't see me working in a hotel or a café."

Gloria stared into the flickering fire, swirling the brandy, warming it in her hand. "Simon," she shifted in the chair now so that she faced him. "Did you say that you'd got the money, you know, to cover renting the shop and what have you?"

"Yeah, I've got some money, from my granddad, he died while I was inside."

He'd been amazed that the will hadn't been changed. He assumed that it was simply that no-one had ever thought about it and for a long time he had toyed with the idea of refusing the bequest. The family, those who were left, had cut him off – they never came to visit. They believed the hype, the newspapers and the judgement and he understood, although it was like a knife in his belly. When it was clear that the will hadn't been contested, which he had fully expected, he decided that it was meant to be. In memory of the times they had enjoyed, the good times in his childhood, he took what was offered. When he came out things would be hard and he would need all the money he could lay his hands on. He was counting his blessings now because with the loss of the storage units up by the dual carriageway the money was going to be essential.

"So, basically, all you need is someone to give you references?"

"Well, yeah, for ordering stuff and so on. I can't buy everything up front I don't think and once people do a credit search, well I wouldn't even be able to get a contract for a bloody mobile phone, I can only have a pay-as-you-go one. What I would need would be someone to rent the shop and sort of front the thing for me. Just to put their name on it for a while you know."

"How do you mean?"

"Well it might work if someone else signed all the papers. It would need to be someone who already had a good reputation, a standing, you know. But it's no good. Hey come on, don't let's spoil the evening with this stuff. Why don't you put on some of that jazz you were playing the other night?"

"Okay." She smiled at him and went to the CD player. The sound of the saxophone and piano filled the room.

When she spoke, it was little more than a whisper, "I'll do that."

"Sorry, I didn't hear you."

She swung round to face him. "I said I'll do that. If you like I can rent the shop in my name, sort out the bank stuff. They know me after all. Let's be clear, I won't give you any money, I want you to understand that up front. I won't go into partnership or anything but if it's just about paperwork and so on, yes I'll do that."

"Bloody hell, Gloria. You can't do that. You don't know me. What are you thinking? You shouldn't even be considering it. No, no, I can't let you. How long have I been here? Just a couple of weeks and you're offering to do that. God, what would your old man say, you really shouldn't be so trusting."

She held up a hand. "I'm not going to argue; I am making this offer once. I won't commit to anything financial and before I do it I want the money in my bank, a sign of goodwill. I'm not as stupid as I might look but, I like you Simon, I reckon I'm a good judge of character and I would like to help you. Whatever you did, you've paid for it now, you've done your time and I'd like to help you get your life going again. Yes, I know most people would think I was crackers but, if you want it, the offer is there. You put some money in my bank, that shows that you trust me, and then I'll rent the shop in my name. Take it or leave it, one time offer. Don't try and answer now, we've both had a bit to drink and this stuff should be done sober."

He put down his glass and slid to the front of the settee. "Gloria, I don't know what to say. I just don't." Now he dropped his head into his hands and hid his face from her.

"Come on, don't go getting all daft on me. Tell me tomorrow if you want to take me up on it."

He stood and crossed the room, pulling her to her feet he wrapped his arms around her and held her in a warm hug. "Thank you, thank you so much." As she raised her face the air between them crackled with tension and he began to lower his head. Suddenly she turned away, pulled from the embrace and bent to tidy the glasses away.

"Right well, early start for me tomorrow so I'll see you at breakfast."

He stopped as he opened the door to leave the room. "Gloria, you've knocked me for six, you really have."

As he climbed the flight of stairs to his room, he couldn't suppress the grin. Stage one had been completed in less time than he could ever have hoped for. He would have his prison. It was in progress, the end game.

Chapter 15

It was worse than he had imagined.

After the agent showed Gloria around she came back with tales of damp and rot. She tried to dissuade him, suggested several other options and even brought brochures. In his mind, though, he had gone too far into the story. He knew the building, assuming there had been no major alterations. It was part of his past and had come to be the only place that could hold the future.

Once they agreed to go ahead he played out in his mind how it would be and now nowhere else would work.

Gloria had eventually given in with a shrug and signed the paperwork. It didn't take long; the owners were amazed to have the chance of rental and didn't want to risk the tenant backing out. In just three weeks she collected the keys and they had gone together to look at it.

The flat upstairs had been long neglected, paper peeled from damp walls and the toilet pan was stained brown, the drains dried out. Bathroom tiles were cracked and dirty and the linoleum curled at the corners. Droppings along the skirtings and in the cupboards evidenced the large rodent population that had made themselves at home.

Gloria tutted and sighed and squealed when a mouse ran from a cupboard in the cramped and dirty kitchen.

"I warned you, Simon, it's pretty awful."

"Oh, it's not as bad as it looks, a good clean and a few coats of paint will make a big difference and I can put new flooring in, change the kitchen cupboards. We did know, didn't we, that it was take it or leave it. I won't do too much to start with, until I see how things go but I can make it habitable. It's cheap, okay you can see why but I think it'll work."

"Well, if you say so. Anyway, I can help you, I have some spare furniture you can borrow for now. I know someone who can fit the flooring for you, cash in hand of course. Could probably even get some carpet if you're not too bothered about the colour. TK Maxx in Harrogate is a great place to get your towels and bedding and what have you."

She was enjoying herself, playing house and it was natural that she would feel involved, so he went along, let her have her moment. There was no harm in it.

The downstairs was in slightly better condition and the layout was pretty much as he remembered. What had been the office at the front and open to the public, was very familiar. A long wooden counter divided the space and he remembered piles of albums holding wedding invitation mock ups, menus and business cards. There had been samples of paper where now were just dirty empty cabinets.

The workshop at the back was what he was really interested in but he didn't loiter there, realising that Gloria wouldn't attach much importance to the big empty space with reinforced concrete floors and the high metal-framed windows. This was where the big presses had been and where he had spent his days earning a reasonable wage; always impatient for a better future but certainly never the one that had taken him, not only from his workplace but from everything he had known or hoped for.

"How's it coming along?" It was now their usual evening routine, the lights dim, jazz playing quietly in the background and each with a glass of alcohol, usually one of her collection of single malts or a brandy to help them unwind. "I wish you'd let me come and see."

He had to be careful now and remember the latest lies. "No, I've told you I want to have a great unveiling when it's all ready."

"You were out a long time today, I wondered where you'd got to."

He nodded, "Time ran away from me. I was painting and stuff."

* * *

He had stood for hours outside the betting shop, down the stinking alley where cat piss and discarded fast food containers scented the air. He had watched Jason Parr enter as he knew he would, as he did almost every day and had done ever since he was able to pass himself off as old enough. People like Jason lived by rote, no imagination to bother them and make them want more and he knew that if he waited they would all arrive. They did, one by one until in the end they were all there, all the gang save one. It had crossed his mind then that he could simply fire bomb the place, throw in a flaming torch and watch them burn. The thought made his hands shake and his eyes water. It would all be over in no time.

That was why it wasn't going to be that way.

He saw them leave in the late afternoon, laughing and pushing at each other as they stormed down the road towards the pub. All older, balder, fatter but still considering themselves cock of the walk.

Afterwards he had gone back to the nasty little shop, had taken out the electric drill and targeted his fury, mounting hooks and rings in the old walls.

The online purchasing had worked well, he'd used the library and even taken the bus into Harrogate and used an internet café there. They would trace him when they had to, he accepted that but by then it wouldn't matter.

* * *

As they sat together in the little lounge he was suddenly aware that soon it would come to an end and Gloria and her kindness would be the only bright thing in a world of darkness and that just a memory.

He walked over and pulled her to her feet. "I'm sorry Gloria but I just can't help it any longer." He lowered his mouth to hers, warm and wanting and felt her body soften as her arms went around his neck to hold the embrace and the kiss to herself. He pulled back. "I've wanted to do that for so long. Is it alright?"

Her eyes shone and she had to blink away the moisture. She didn't speak but pulled him closer, wrapping her arms around his neck. She returned the kiss then drew back and turned away. But she took his hand in hers and led him out into the narrow hallway that led to the bedroom. Inside the room he hugged her to him again and they fell backwards onto the bed with her beneath him half on the mattress, her legs bent over the edge. Now he raised his hand and stroked away the strands of hair that had fallen across her face. She shuffled backwards and spun round to lay beside him, their heads on the heaped pillows. His fingers moved to the buttons of her blouse and as he pushed them through the tiny button holes he felt her hands on his belt, on his zip.

Afterwards, in the dark of her room, warm in bed with her spooned against him breathing deeply, he was flooded with guilt. He hadn't meant this to happen and as he'd felt the attraction grow he had fought it back. If he hadn't needed her to be a front for him, he would have left weeks ago. If he hadn't had to use her, he would have moved on and forgotten the kindness and friendship. His quiet murmur was lost in the pillow, "I'm sorry Gloria. I am, I'm sorry." She didn't stir and he knew she would come to hate him in time but he had told her, in his heart he knew he had told her.

* * *

She was attentive the next morning. Dressed in a cream silk dressing gown, slim and attractive with dark hair loose around her shoulders, she brought him tea in bed. When her own drink was finished, she stood and then turned to look down at him propped against the pillows, dishevelled and unshaven and she smiled. "Well, I can't say it was a surprise, Simon, but though the waiting wasn't unpleasant, I'm glad we've got here in the end." And with a cheeky grin she turned and left the room.

Moments later he heard the shower and he squeezed his eyes shut and fought with shame and self-disgust. Then he made himself remember, he forced himself to think of another girl with long dark hair and shining eyes, a gentle smile. He thought of Sandie and she chased away the regret.

Chapter 16

Stephen Hardcastle had gone to work on the buses straight from school and was now part of the furniture. He trailed to work from the tiny terraced house where he had lived with his mother until her death. Back home at the end of each shift he spent his evenings slumped in front of the television or had an occasional night at the pub or afternoon in the bookies when his shifts allowed it. He had been simple to find and it took no time to work out his narrow, wasted life. Simon remembered the working schedules from way back. They had used the knowledge to blag free rides and 'Stevo' had swelled with pride and feeble power, waving his hand at them as the gang climbed off the bus with mumbled thanks. Puffed up at the opportunity to dispense favours he never imagined that he was being used.

The chances were that shift timings had changed in the intervening years, so Simon watched. From the street in the early morning, from the little café in time for the three o'clock start and from the pub in the evening. The waitress in the café began to smile at him when he came in, he had become a regular but it didn't matter. She would probably only ever remember the heavy framed glasses, bought from the local chemist, the mildest reading glasses they had. She may remember the fact that he always wore a yellow scarf and spoke with a stammer. Anything to muddy the waters, in case they looked for him before it was all over. A shy sort of chap she would say when asked, but no she hadn't noticed a scar, well he always had his head down didn't he, wouldn't look you in the eye. The subterfuge wouldn't need to last very long, just long enough.

The rota was simple and now he was ready. Stephen was on afternoons and so would finish after the last bus. The eleven thirty to the railway station was back in the garage by twelve.

Simon rang Gloria, "I'm stuck at the shop waiting for a delivery and he's held up on the motorway. I think I'll just hang about and then have something to eat at the pub. It could be late, I don't want to disturb you, I'll sleep in my own room."

"I don't mind, just come in when you get back."

"It could be very late."

"It's okay, really it won't matter." He recognised the closeness now for the mistake it was but there was no choice at this stage but to accommodate it. He tried to put a smile in his voice.

"Okay then. See you later. Don't wait up though, eh."

* * *

It was cold and there was a fine drizzle falling. Orange mist swirled around the street lamps and dark pools gleamed in the gutters, a filthy night.

Simon slid into the narrow alley between the second-hand car showroom and the church hall, and waited for the bulky figure to waddle up the hill. In the years since he had last seen him, hours sitting in the driving seat, too many burgers and a love of beer had spread Hardcastle's backside and belly, and wasted the muscles of his arms and legs. He was starting with the softest target but it didn't matter where it began.

Cars hissed past throwing up the standing water and now and again someone would hustle along the road, head lowered and shoulders hunched but it was quiet enough.

When the dark shape appeared round the corner Simon slid his hand into the inside pocket of his new puffa jacket. The handle on the hammer was smooth and warmed by the heat of his body. Dark steel gleamed in the subdued light. His hand was steady.

The sound surprised him, he had thought it would be louder, sharper. There was just a quiet thunk, and then the slither of bulk falling to the wet pavement, the crack of his skull as it hit the floor was the loudest sound. Simon had intended to catch him as he fell but his reaction was actually to step away. It was over quickly. The quick emergence from the alley, the hammer's arc, connection and a barely audible gasp. He dragged the dead weight along the grimy pavement and into the dark mouth of the ginnel. He stopped and crouched in the wet, lowered his head towards the gaping mouth and listened. The hiss of rain and the gurgle of water in the downspouts and gutters obliterated any sound of breathing. Lack of light and the bulk of Hardcastle's jacket made it impossible to tell whether the chest still rose and fell.

He pushed fingers under the dark collar, felt the sticky warmth of blood as it pooled in the fat creases. It had been guesswork, if he had struck too hard then this pig would be dead already. He didn't want him dead.

He felt the faint flutter of life and allowed himself a smile. It took longer than he had imagined to wrap the tape round and round the wrists and ankles, the calves and thighs. By the time he had finished, Hardcastle was groaning quietly. He pressed a wad of rag into his mouth and secured it with a piece of tape.

He was heavy and awkward and Simon had to stop twice and rest with his back against the dripping wall before he eventually dragged him through the alley.

The old van had been nicked the night before from a second-hand car place, out beyond the down-at-heel area where his shop was. It had spent the intervening time hidden in the yard, tucked up against the walls of the workshop. An old door thrown inside just before he left was essential now to enable him to drag the still unresponsive body up and into the dirty interior. He had imagined it was going to be difficult but hadn't realised just how cumbersome the unconscious hulk would be and by the time he dropped onto the torn plastic of the driver's seat he was clammy with sweat and gasping for breath. It was only half over and he needed to move fast now before Hardcastle regained his senses.

The route round the back roads and alleys to avoid the ubiquitous CCTV cameras took longer than planned and by the time they were nearly there he could hear his captive shuffling and thumping in the back of the van. He didn't want to hit him again, didn't want to risk him dying but nevertheless as he parked back in the yard he pulled the hammer out of his jacket and held it ready as he unfastened the rusty back doors. Hardcastle was still lying in the middle of the van floor but his eyes were open now. As the light level increased he tried to raise himself up, thrusting with his legs, pushing and squirming, furious and confused.

"Hello Stevo, it's me." Simon clambered into the back of the van and watched as the fury and confusion were obliterated by fear.

Chapter 17

Simon brandished the hammer as he clambered into the back of the van. Hardcastle cowered before him. The overfed face was streaked with blood and now tears caused drying streaks to thin and run down across his cheeks and drip from his wobbling chins onto his dark jacket. He tried to speak, gag and tape notwithstanding and the guttural gurgling made him even more pathetic.

Simon crouched alongside. He put down the hammer and watched the look of relief spark in the piggy eyes. Simon didn't turn away, he wanted to see the reaction as he lifted the butcher knife from the tool box fixed to the side of the van. It was all it he could have wished for, absolute unbridled terror. The fat man shook his head, tears and sweat flying across the space to land on Simon's jacket, he wiped spots from his face. Hardcastle flailed desperately with his bound legs, pushing against the chipboard flooring in a frantic attempt to create some distance between himself and the gleaming steel blade.

Simon leaned forward, his mouth so close that his lips touched the tip of Hardcastle's ears as he hissed out a warning. "We are getting out now. If you try anything clever I will kill you, I will stick this into your fat gut and leave your innards in the yard. Do you understand me?"

He nodded desperately, terrified mumbles escaped from around the gag. Simon pulled his captive up and then, standing behind, and kicking and nudging with his feet, pushed him across the van to the open exit.

As Hardcastle swung his legs round to hang over the edge of the space Simon kicked out viciously forcing the bound body to tumble forwards where it landed with a sickening smack on the cracked concrete of the yard. He jumped down and leaned over the snivelling hulk.

Although he had tried to curl and turn his head as he fell, Hardcastle's nose had smashed into the hard concrete. Yet more blood flowed downwards soaking the already sopping jumper and jacket. Simon dragged the semiconscious man upwards. He slit the parcel tape binding his feet and pressed the knife to his neck. A small red bead formed, became a thread and the thin stream slid under the collar and down inside jacket and shirt. Hardcastle was frozen with fear, snorting in anguish, the whites of his eyes flashing pink in the glow from the rear lights of the car. He was breathing rapidly through his nose and gobbets of blood streaked snot bubbled out.

"Keep still arsehole. Don't move a muscle until I tell you."

The bindings on Hardcastle's knees held. Simon pulled him up by the back of his jacket and, holding the knife against his neck and kicking at the stumbling feet, shuffled him forward towards the warehouse door. Tiny baby steps made ridiculous by the bulk of the man.

Once they were close enough Simon reached past the sobbing form and pushed open the door. He hadn't bothered to lock it. After tonight he would need to be more careful about security though. Holding the knife down by his side now he used his other hand to push Hardcastle through the opening and send him sprawling across the floor.

He laid the knife on the narrow window ledge and then bent to grab the back of the filthy busman's uniform jacket. "Over here, you fat pig, come on, move."

Hardcastle was sliding away into unconsciousness, whether from fear or the blow on the head Simon couldn't tell, he didn't care. He manhandled the almost unconscious body towards the wall, kicking out to make him roll and shuffle across the space. Eventually he was close enough.

Simon reached up and dragged down the length of chain fastened to rings in the wall. He closed the shackles around the ankles and then slit the tape on Hardcastle's wrists. He dragged his hands forward, threaded a second chain through rings welded to the old plates in the floor that had supported the printing presses. He closed the wrist cuffs and secured them all using the keys that had been provided.

He hadn't believed it would be possible to buy such things so easily but had found everything is available online.

He had bought a tablet computer and used hot spots, hotels, MacDonald's car parks. He used VPNs and blessed the hours he had spent in the computer suites in the various jails. So, the thing kept warning him that his browsing wasn't secure, it didn't matter. The worst that could happen was someone could hack his bank account but most of the money was in the new one he had created with Gloria. He trickle-fed the old one when he needed cash. He would draw out what he needed from one ATM and then use the details of the new one to deposit the funds in the machines in another branch. It was clumsy and time consuming but it worked. Apart from the fact that he needed the money, it would look odd to Gloria if the new account was static when he was giving her constant updates of his progress setting up the business. Ultimately there would be a virtual trail back to him but not until people began to investigate what was happening.

He picked up an old towel bought along with a heap of other stuff at the charity shop, sloshed water onto the balding head and then wiped the muck from Hardcastle's face. He threw a blanket across his legs and made sure the bucket was within reach.

"I'll be back later arsehole." He turned away, collected his knife and walked out of the room, locked and bolted all three new locks on the heavy door and then clambered back into the van. He drove out onto the moor where he set fire to the stolen vehicle and waited until he was sure there would be little left. Just another case of vandalism.

The walk back to Mill Lodge in the quiet starlight was magical, he listened to the owl and the sigh of the wind over the hills and let his nerves settle. He climbed quietly up the stairs and took a long shower, put his filthy wet clothes into a bin bag and then went down to the living quarters at the back. Maybe Gloria would still be awake, or maybe she would wake as he wrapped his arms around her. Despite the walk, he was buzzing and didn't think he would sleep; he needed some sort of release for the adrenaline. He slid into the warm bed and nuzzled the back of her neck.

Chapter 18

Darkness and violence filled his early morning mind. Back in his own room memory of what had happened was unreal. Just a couple of miles away a bruised and battered Stephen Hardcastle had spent the night chained to the walls of a filthy workshop.

Cold sweat broke out on Simon's forehead, turned his body clammy under the covers.

For all the years inside this had been his answer. Brutality and death to repay the evil that had shattered his life and stolen his future. His mouth dried as a shocking rush of self-doubt overwhelmed him. There was something else; he knew it wasn't fear. For him the worst had already happened and there was nothing further to fear.

Slashed and hacked and left to bleed to death in the grubby shower. Picked out because of what he was, the lowest of the low in the prison pecking order – a child killer. Expecting it constantly for weeks and then, with the feel of a sharpened screwdriver against his neck, he hadn't been afraid. He had welcomed the chance of escape from memories of the past and despair for the future. When his blood had flowed across grimy tiles into the drains, he had slipped into the peace of acceptance. Afterwards, in the calm of the hospital wing, he had cursed the people who had found him, saved him. But he had survived and *the plan* had been the only thing that had kept him going, kept him sane. It had filled his eyes with anger and made him untouchable and unapproachable no matter where they had sent him.

He tossed and turned in the sleep-warmed bed. If it wasn't fear, then what was causing the sickness in his stomach and the clutch at his heart which took his breath?

It was doubt, after all this time. Not doubt about the justice of it but doubt that he could carry it through to the end and there was shame. He threw back the covers, panic pushed him from the bed. The foundations of his hate were crumbling, he had never before questioned that he had the strength to do this and yet here it was.

He didn't want to kill. The violence of yesterday had not brought him peace, he felt no satisfaction in the memory of Hardcastle snivelling and terrified.

He had never intended to walk away after it was over. Coming back had always been the end game but now, on the edges of the moor breathing the untainted air, walking alone across the tops and then coming back to share the nights with Gloria, her arms warm around him, her breath on his cheek and her smile filling his eyes, he wanted more.

Letting life back in had been a mistake. How much did he want it and which did he want most? Revenge and death or something else, softer and kinder. One thing was sure there could be no future unless he stepped back now and if he found Hardcastle dead this morning – well then it was already too late.

He slumped on the end of the bed and lowered his head. He couldn't think straight. He had expected some sort of satisfaction by now but he could only find disgust at himself, anguish and self-loathing.

He could stop it. Yes, he had beaten and battered his victim but he had stopped short of the ultimate act. There was still time. He had control, he had power.

There was still the chance to wash his hands of it, of this place and go, find a way to make a life, an existence that would take him through the decades until it was time to die.

He staggered to the bathroom. In the shower, hot water pounding onto his head, he fought with his conscience. He thumped out at the wall and bit back the howl of frustration that built in his throat.

"Shit!"

Incredibly here they were – second thoughts, after all the certainty. It appeared that the starting of it, the long awaited, planned for and prayed for beginning had twisted round and instead of making him empowered, it had all begun to slip away.

When he closed his eyes the sight of Hardcastle's face bleeding and broken and the sound of the blood bubbling in his ruined nose came back. He swallowed the nausea as the truth grew. He saw that he couldn't carry on with it, he couldn't do it twice more, Robert Parker was to have been next and then the last would have been Jason Parr. He wouldn't be able to take it through to the end. He couldn't kill. Not in cold blood.

Why they had made him the scapegoat had never been clear. He had called them his friends, these men who were boys with him, but he had never been as confident or daring and so they weeded him out and sacrificed him.

He had been seen, waiting near the park. He'd admitted that. When the police questioned him, endlessly he had said that. He told them he had been angry that night. His girlfriend had finished with him, wouldn't even talk about why and instead of drowning his sorrow in the pub, with his mates, the way it should be, here he was hanging about waiting for Sandie to come back from her training. He'd become bored waiting. Boredom, had been his crime he'd said, boredom and fury at Tracey. So, he had stalked away, out to the hills to fume and vent. He thought Sandie would be fine, it wasn't even dark, she would be fine, nothing could happen to her. But it had, evil had come and taken her innocence and left her to die in the fading light of a late summer day. Then his mates had told the police they expected him in the pub but he hadn't turned up. They painted him as different, a loner, never quite one of them, odd, weird. They had sowed the seeds of suspicion and helped to serve him up.

Now the strength left his legs and he sank to the floor under the pounding water. He had seen them, in the gallery at the court, watched them in the witness box, betraying him – handing him over.

He lowered his head to his knees, roiling emotion drove the breath from his body, left him gasping in the cooling steam. Here, for the first time since the police had fastened the handcuffs and he had looked up to see Jason Parr's sneering face in the back of the crowd he experienced doubt.

He stepped from the shower and dried his shivering body, pulled on jeans and sweater and turned to look out of the window at the early mist on the moors and felt his life fall apart for the second time.

* * *

Gloria was preparing breakfast for the little family who were waiting noisily in the dining room. "Don't bother with mine Gloria. I've got to get off, loads to do today and I have to go into Leeds."

"Oh hello, dormouse, I thought you'd died."

She didn't know how close she had come to the truth. He was dead inside, the pulse of hate that had kept him going had fled, leaving him emptied out like a coconut shell. He dredged up a smile, put on the false face that he wore with her.

She had been happy for him to keep the room upstairs but most nights for the last couple of weeks they sat together in the quiet lounge before moving through to her feminine bedroom where sex had begun as a careful journey of discovery but now was relaxed and fun. Time out for both of them in lives that were hard living. When there were guests, as now, he would go to his own room in the early hours, a guest again – nothing more.

* * *

"Right, you going for your meeting?"

Yet more code and obfuscation, making things what they were not.

"Yeah. I'm going straight to the shop after. Have a lovely day. Maybe we should get a take-away tonight." Though he was shredded inside he made his mouth smile.

"No, I'll cook us something, I'm here all day anyway, more guests arriving this afternoon."

"Oh, okay – I'll bring a bottle of wine then."

She turned her head up for a kiss and watched as he left by the back door, tapping at the window on his way down the narrow side passage.

He should go straight to Leeds but instead he rang from the station.

"Chris, can I come later? I missed the bloody bus and they are only one an hour unless I change three times."

He heard the gust of a sigh on the other end of the line. "Bloody hell, Simon, I hope you're not going to make a habit of this. You have to stick to the appointments. Look I'll make you one for tomorrow, in the afternoon. That'll give you plenty of time to get yourself here. Half three, don't be late."

These scheduled meetings with the probation officers were an integral part of his licence conditions. He had been to one already inside the prison, immediately before his release. He had met Chris, who could barely wipe the boredom from his face. They were pointless and useless. Time filled with lies, listening to this official who had no idea what his life really was, what his plans were. It had to be done so he put on the act. It would cause major problems if he didn't turn up. He believed he knew just how the conversation would go. Chris would want to know if he wouldn't consider moving away. He had told him he wanted to be "home", that he needed to be somewhere familiar. Chris wanted him to toe the line, wanted him in Leeds or Manchester, wanted him anonymous and invisible. Chris wanted his life easy. He knew he would be told, yet again that he should sign on for Job Seeker's Allowance, though he had said repeatedly that he was determined to find some work. He knew that they all thought he had no idea what he was talking about, no clue as to what it would be like. Well, he couldn't give Chris and his colleagues what they wanted and it was them who had no idea.

He would bite his tongue and keep calm, it would tie knots in his gut but there was no other option. He would promise to be careful, to keep his head down and stay out of trouble.

It was all a complete waste of time that he could well do without, especially now.

He swallowed his impatience and kept his tone even. "Thanks, thanks so much. I'll see you tomorrow."

* * *

As he walked up the hill towards the shop and the mess that was waiting for him, his stomach was churning. He would make Stephen Hardcastle tell him why. The fat slob had been scared of him right from the off and the beating, the threats had made him a quivering wreck. He would force him to confess the truth of it, the whole of it and then he would decide. Who deserved punishment, and for what and when. It was his decision to make but first he would have the facts. He should have done it this way right from the start, he saw that now. This was honourable.

Chapter 19

It was cold and rain threatened, the sweatshirt wasn't enough. He would need to go shopping. It was ludicrous given what he was dealing with, but the jacket had been too badly stained to wear and there hadn't been time yet to replace it. Any new one would need to be the same as the sopping, filthy one that he had thrown into the skip. He didn't know how much Gloria noticed but splashing out on clothes when he was supposed to be pouring all his money into a new business would look a bit odd.

Okay, he could do that – it would be easy, a new jacket, jeans, some new trainers to replace the ones that were covered in splatters of blood and mud. First though, he must deal with what waited for him in the old shop.

He unlocked the hefty padlocks on the yard gate and stepped over broken concrete towards the warehouse. There was no sound. He pushed open the door, "Stevo, it's me."

The smell hit him, "Bloody hell, have you pissed yourself?" Light leaking in from the open door fell across the battered hulk laying in a liquid nightmare, proof that Hardcastle had lost control in the darkness. Simon's gut clenched, did this mean that his captive had died in the night? His eyes were barely visible behind discoloured and swollen lids. There was no movement in the podgy limbs and Simon hovered at the doorway, unsure what to do. Then he heard a low groan. The relief he felt was proof positive, if he had still needed it, that he had stepped back from the abyss. He knelt beside the stinking man.

Hardcastle sensed the presence beside him and began to whimper and groan as he tried to raise his hands, to protect his face or hide from what might be coming it was difficult to say. It was too great an effort in any case and his arms flopped back to his side. He turned his head and the muscles in his face worked with the effort of trying to open the engorged lids.

Simon lifted a bottle of water to the cracked and crusted lips. As he tipped it into Hardcastle's mouth liquid ran down his chin and along the folds of fat above his collar but some of the drink trickled in and his throat moved as he swallowed.

The butcher knife was still in his hand but Simon saw now that he didn't need it. He walked over to the narrow window ledge and placed it on the cracked tile. A pile of old cloths was in the corner, he grabbed some from the top of the heap and wet them under the cold tap over the ancient sink.

As he sponged the blood and muck from Hardcastle's face the broken man began to revive. He kicked out with his legs and tried to grab at Simon, guttural sounds of panic and fear growing as adrenaline gave him feeble strength. The chains jangled and clanked with each movement.

"Okay, okay Stephen. Just calm down now. Just keep still, yeah. Can you hear me, keep still?" The words made little difference and Simon had to grab out at the now feebly flailing hands. "Okay, either you stop fighting me or I'll hurt you again, it's up to you."

The struggle ceased. The recent panic caused bleeding to start again and Simon wiped it away and poured more water into the other man's mouth which opened now as he gulped and coughed.

It was too late to do anything about the soiled clothes and it was impossible to remove them without taking off the shackles and so Simon kicked the sopping blanket away and replaced it with another.

"You know who I am don't you Stephen?" For a moment there was no sound, no movement save the whistle of breath through blocked nostrils. Simon kicked out at the fat legs under the tartan cover. "I said you know who I am, don't you?"

Hardcastle nodded.

"Right, next question. You know why I'm here, don't you?" There was nothing, no movement, no sound. "You need to answer me, you really do. You need to get out of here and back home. I can make that happen. I can take you home Stephen. You'd like that, wouldn't you?" There was still nothing.

Kneeling in front of Hardcastle, who had begun to whimper again and was shaken with spasms of shivering that caused yet more groans, he spoke low and quiet. "I'll ask again, you know why I'm here, don't you Stephen? You have to tell me the truth, you need to tell me everything and then I might let you go. Do you understand? I'm going to make it easy for you. I am going to ask you simple questions and you can give me straightforward answers. Don't lie to me Stephen. I will know if you lie to me – okay?"

The snivelling man nodded just once as tears trickled down his face.

Simon had to go back to the very start. His new thinking hadn't gone as far as any sort of forgiveness, he would never forget but he still needed confirmation of all he believed.

Deep down there was a sense of peace that he hadn't expected. He would not kill, not now and maybe not ever. It was as if yet another prison had released him. It wasn't over, a new phase had begun.

For all of these years he had blanked the detail, apart from the desperate denials, first to the police when they had shown him photographs and forced him to look and then in court when he had yelled out "No!" over and over until he collapsed and was taken away.

For years locked in and alone he had pushed the darkness back. Tried to replace the images of Sandie, pale and destroyed in the long grass with memories of her running, whole and free at her sports meetings. Now though, now he had to let it through because unless he faced it all he couldn't speak about it.

He closed his eyes and drew in a deep breath.

Sitting on an old box he leaned towards Hardcastle who was calmer now. "So Stevo, here we are. I bet you thought you'd never see me again, didn't you?"

There was a snuffle and the body shifted, trying to find some comfort. "Tell you what, let's have a plan. You answer my questions, you tell me what I want to hear and for each answer I'll give you a little prize. How do you like that idea? Just nod Stevo, no need to speak. Not yet anyway."

There was no response and it seemed that maybe the fat man had drifted into unconsciousness. Simon shook his shoulders. "Did you hear me fatso? Shit you really have let yourself go. Mind, you were always a bit of a pig, weren't you?" Hardcastle moved, he nodded just once.

"Excellent, so you are a pig, well that got that out of the way."

"No."

"Ah, so you can speak. Brilliant. So, we can move right along. It's all very easy really. I want to know whose idea it was to drop me in it."

Hardcastle tensed now and tried to draw up his knees, the chains rattled and clinked together and when he had pulled his feet as far as they would go he pushed back on his behind, trying to sit up.

"Okay, don't get agitated. First thing. You tell me who decided I was going to be the fall guy and I'll make you more comfortable, I'll get those stinking pants off you for a start. Do we have a deal?"

He shook his head now back and forth, back and forth.

Simon fought the urge to strike. "That's not going to get us very far. I want to help you Stevo. I'll be honest, I wanted to hurt you, I was going to kill you." There was another whimper of fear. "But I've had second thoughts and now, well now I don't want to hurt you anymore. I want to clean you up, take you home. I can put you in your nice comfy bed. You'd like that wouldn't you, Stevo – a nice clean bed, some soup? Tell you what, I'll make it even easier. Was it that bastard Parr? He always did call the tune. Did he put you up to it? You could have kept your mouths shut. You could have just said you didn't know where I was. Whose idea was it to point the cops towards me? Just me. I'm waiting arsehole."

Hardcastle found the strength to shake his head firmly back and forth, the movement obviously painful and difficult.

"But somebody did, didn't they? Somebody twisted things and heaped it all on me. Somebody planted my sweater there with her and I think you know who." Now there was just the drip of water in the yard outside and the click and creak of wood swelling in the feeble sunlight. "Shit, come on Stephen." Still nothing. Hardcastle's fists clenched and unclenched on his thighs causing the links in the chain to clink. He breathed heavily through his mouth, agitation building.

"Okay, you don't want to talk to me that's fine. Forget it. Do you think I haven't got other ideas? Do you think I can't do this without you? I've had a long time to stew over this mate, a long, long time. You don't want to help me, fair enough. I'll just walk out of here now, lock the door and forget you. I wonder how long it's going to be before they notice you're missing. I rang the bus depot by the way, told them how poorly you are with that nasty stomach bug, they won't miss you for at least a week. The others, Jason, Robert, do you think they're going to come looking for you? Do you? You're a fool if you do, do you think they care about you? You saw how much they cared about me, well didn't you? I wonder how long you'll last. Huh, could be a while living off your fat but then again with no water... hmm not sure. I'll be long gone anyway so I'll just have to wait to read it in the paper, read all about how a body's been found, chewed by rats, slowly liquefying in this filthy place. That's what happens you know, your skin splits and your insides leak out, course you won't know about that, you'll be well dead by then." He stood and stepped back, "So, that's your decision? You're gonna die for them. Well I'm sure they'll be really grateful."

"Tommy, don't Tommy!" The pleading was no more than a whisper pushed from between swollen lips which began to bleed again.

"Oh my God, what the hell!" Simon spun at the shrill shout to see Gloria, her hands pressed to her face, her eyes huge and terrified, standing at the open door of the workshop with her husband's jacket in a heap at her feet.

Chapter 20

Simon took a step towards the open door trying to block her view as Gloria leaned to peer past him into the grim interior. Stephen Hardcastle was slumped against the wall. "What the hell are you doing? How did you get in?"

"Down the back alley, the side gate. It doesn't matter!"

"I didn't know there was a back alley."

She screeched at him, "I said it doesn't bloody matter. What the hell is this?"

Simon turned his head to glance at the mess behind him, he didn't know how to begin. In the time he took, Gloria reached out and picked up the butcher knife.

"No, it's okay, you don't need to do that – really you don't, it's okay."

Fear came from her in waves, fear and anger. "Okay? How can this be okay?" She had taken several steps into the room by now and was an arm's length away from where Simon stood, struggling for words.

"It's not as bad as it looks." He stopped, he sounded ludicrous. He reached a hand towards her. She raised the knife. "Why are you here Gloria, why have you come?"

"You didn't bring a coat, I watched you walk down the alley and then it began to rain. I brought a coat." Tears filled her eyes as she spoke to him, she brushed them away with her free hand and glanced around. "You haven't done anything. You haven't decorated, where's all the stuff that you ordered? It's just the same."

Any answer that he might make was negated by a bout of coughing from behind him. Gloria slid past, still holding the knife in front of her. She flicked her glance between the semi-conscious man sagging against the wall and Simon who raised his hands, palms towards her in helplessness and surrender.

She knelt now beside Hardcastle who appeared to be drifting in and out of consciousness. "Bloody hell, what happened to him?" She glanced up. "He stinks, he's wet himself. We need to get him to the hospital, we need an ambulance. What happened to his head? He's got concussion or something." She reached out to take Stephen's hand and it was only then that she noticed the cuffs, the chains. "What the hell!" She pulled at them, jangling and shaking the metal links. "My God, what have you done? What the hell have you done?"

"I can explain, I can. I'll tell you all about it. It's not what you think."

"How the hell do you know what I think – Christ even I don't even know what I think! Who is this, who is this bloke?"

A faint whisper slipped between Hardcastle's lips, "Help me, please. Don't let him kill me, don't leave me."

"Shush, shush, it's okay. Don't worry I'm not leaving you. I'm going to get you an ambulance."

"No. No don't – just take me home. I'll be okay if you just take me home." Simon had moved forward to stand beside Gloria, she still gripped the big knife and raised it as she leaned back to peer up at him.

"I can explain Gloria. I was going to take him home. I just needed him to tell me first."

"Tell you what?"

"Can we talk later? Look I'll get him home now."

"How?"

"What do you mean?"

"How are you going to get him home? Are you going to ring a taxi, are you going to take him on the bus? Look at the state of him."

"I need a van, I was going to go and…"

"Ah, just going to go and get a van, and some poor sod was going to have his vehicle stolen."

"Well, I hadn't expected to be doing this now. Look I know it looks bad, shit it is bad, of course it is but let me try to explain."

"Tommy, Tommy take me home – please."

"He's delirious, he doesn't know who we are. We really need to get him to the hospital."

"No, he's not delirious. It's me. I'm Tommy. They changed my name, when I came out."

"Oh, oh okay. Yeah of course they did. So, you're Tommy – Tommy Fulton or…"

"Webb, I'm Tommy Webb." He watched as she sifted through her memory, saw recognition dawn and listened as she whispered his name.

"Tommy Webb – Sandie Webb's brother."

There was nothing for him to do now but to nod and give her space to let the knowledge sink in.

The silence stretched between them until it was broken by another groan from Hardcastle as he tried to push himself into a more comfortable position.

Gloria turned to him and then spun her head back towards Simon. She jagged the knife at him. "Go and stand in the corner. Does this thing," she reached and jangled the chain, "have any keys or whatever, how do I get them off him?"

"I've got them, here let me."

"Don't try anything, I will slash you, just move slowly. Unfasten him."

"It's okay, honestly Gloria, it's okay. I won't hurt him. I won't hurt you. I promise."

"Unfasten him then. Unfasten him and then take those stinking clothes off him.

"Right, right. Okay."

The job was nasty and difficult but in the end Hardcastle was laid on top of the blankets with towels wrapped around him. The blood had been wiped from his face and though he still shook with tremors, he was calm.

Simon kicked the wet and stinking clothes towards the wall.

"No, pick 'em up."

"What?"

"Pick those up and stick 'em in that plastic bag."

"There's no need. I can sort them out later."

"Either pick them up now or you're going to have to sit in that mess."

Simon shook his head, his face creased in puzzlement until Gloria's plan became clear. "Sit in the... No, look Gloria there's no need. Honestly, I promise I won't hurt you, I won't hurt him."

She jagged the knife at him, "Move the mess and then sit down. Give me the keys for those things, what are they, shackles? Cuffs? Anyway, it doesn't matter, just give me the keys." He held them out towards her.

"You don't need to, really." But as he spoke he kicked the things together and then, bundled them into a bag.

"Sit down."

He turned and began to speak again but as she stood before him, her legs braced and the knife held at arm's length, he just shook his head and lowered to the floor.

"Right, put those things on your feet."

He clicked on the shackles. She threw the key to him. "Lock them."

"Gloria, please. Look, I promise I'll stay here. I won't move unless you tell me to." She stopped, began to take stock of the whole situation. She realised that leaning towards him and forcing his hands into the cuffs and then locking them afterwards was going to be too dangerous and probably impossible for her to achieve.

He saw confusion now in her eyes and the wrinkle of the skin on her brow. "Gloria, let me help you, let me help you get him home."

She glanced down at the other man, the bulk of him, his semi-conscious state.

"Okay, okay. My car is in the road. Where is the key for this place?"

"It's here in my pocket." She held out her hand.

Her choices were limited but the main thing was to get help for the injured man. "I'm going to get the car." She ran from the room now and they heard the locks thumping into place. Hardcastle whimpered, now that he was alone with Simon, the fear resurging.

"It's alright Stephen, you've been bloody lucky. She'll help you now."

He could take her. He could hide behind the door and when she came back in, he could have her in a heartbeat but Simon sat on the floor and listened as her car rumbled into the yard. He waited until Gloria came back, holding the knife before her, a wrench from the car's toolbox another weapon in her other hand.

She kicked open the door and let it bounce against the wall and only when she saw that he was still on the floor did she move into the room.

"Right let's get him to the hospital. Help me take him to the car."

"No, not the hospital. I don't want to go to the hospital." Hardcastle knew the hospital would involve the police and he obviously wanted to avoid it at all costs. "Take me home."

"You can't go home." She turned her head, "who is it, what's his name?"

"Stephen, Stephen Hardcastle."

"Look Stephen you can't go home. Tell you what why don't I take you back to my place."

"Yes, oh yes please." He reached out and gripped her hand, he was obviously becoming stronger and at the end of the day it was his choice.

"Okay, come on let's get you in the car. We'll go back to my place. Come on Simon, give me a hand, but I've still got this, and I'll use it." She waved the knife in the air in front of her.

"It's okay, Gloria, I promise. It's okay. I'll help you now."

Chapter 21

Between them they carried and dragged Hardcastle to the car. Gloria opened the hatchback and spread a couple of travel rugs over the floor. They laid him down curled awkwardly into the confined space.

"Lock the shop doors, I need you to help me at the other end, otherwise there is no way you would get anywhere near my car. When we get back you pack your stuff and get out – do you understand?"

"Gloria, give me a chance, will you. Let me explain. I'll move out, of course I will but please let me tell you what I did, why I did it."

"I liked you, Simon, or Tommy, whatever the hell you're called. I liked you. Just goes to show what an idiot I still am."

There was no point right now trying to explain. His plans, his resolve had changed so much and so recently that Simon didn't have the words anyway. He had thought he would just use her to front his purchase of the premises, he had thought he didn't care. The plan now seemed ridiculous, renting a shop, his old workplace. What was that for, it seemed to be like something he had read, dreamt maybe and it was so hard to believe that this had been his only reason for everything he had done since he had been released.

Since he had known that he wasn't going to kill them a nub of humanity had opened in him and began the unfurling of a desire to make things better. He wanted to leave all the hate behind. He still had a burning need to find out what had happened, why people had behaved the way that they had, but not in the way that he had intended. More than that he had enjoyed the time with Gloria. Her openness and giving nature had gentled the anger and made him want more than bloody revenge and then his own suicide. She had made him want to live.

Gloria climbed into the driver's seat leaving the door open and resting one foot on the ground outside. She still held the knife pointing awkwardly at Simon, but they both knew now that she wasn't going to need it. She took out her phone and, unexpectedly typed a text. She fiddled awkwardly keeping the handset in her left hand, clicking away at the tiny keys with her thumb, glancing down briefly as she worked.

"This is a text to my mate. It's got your name in it, both your soddin' names and that you have beaten this bloke up. When that gets to your probation officer you can kiss your licence goodbye. You move towards me in any way and I'm pressing send, I can do it in an instant. Understand?"

He nodded at her, impressed, it had been a good move. He pushed as far to the left-hand side as he could with his hands clasped together on his lap.

"I won't hurt you Gloria, I promise."

She threw the knife into the corner of the yard, slammed the door and started the car, reversed out into the road with the phone still clutched in her right hand her thumb hovering over the send button.

"Can I lock the yard?"

"No."

They were back at the little hotel in ten minutes and she drove into her garage. "Right, I can't risk anyone seeing him, I've got guests. You stay here with him. I know you can run but if you do I will make it my duty to have the police here, I'll tell them what you did. It won't matter what this bloke says or doesn't say." She leaned into the back of the car and took four or five photographs of Stephen Hardcastle, his battered face and the bruises, livid and nasty on his back and belly and the blood crusted wound on his head from the hammer. "Don't move – right?"

He nodded at her as she held up the phone and rushed down the narrow side path to the back door.

Chapter 22

Hardcastle was recovering visibly and by the time Gloria reappeared, carrying an overcoat and some slippers he was peering out of the rear window.

"Where's this, what's going on? I can't afford no hotel."

"No, it's okay Stephen, this is my place." She had opened the hatchback and Simon walked round to help her get him out.

She draped the overcoat around his shoulders and bent to slide the slippers onto his feet.

"Everyone is out just now so let's just get him inside. We're putting him in the room on the ground floor – the disabled one."

The room was warm and clean. The door was larger than would be normal to allow access for wheelchairs, they squeezed in three abreast.

Gloria whisked the coat away and flung it in the corner. "Do you think you could manage a shower if we help you? It would make you more comfortable I think."

Hardcastle was moving carefully, trying to hold his head steady, favouring his left arm and limping but he nodded at her and then put out a hand to steady himself. They eased him towards the bathroom.

"Help him will you Simon, there's a seat in the shower and what have you."

"Me?"

She didn't answer but the glance demanded compliance. She made up the bed and by the time he came out clean and pink from the warm water he was looking much better. "Get him into bed, I'm going through to the kitchen to warm up some soup."

* * *

Later, while Hardcastle snored, Gloria whispered to Simon standing in the middle of her living room. "I think he's got concussion and I don't like the look of all that bruising, you can get a ruptured spleen you know, that can kill you."

"I think he would have been dead by now."

"That's horrible. I still think we should get him into hospital."

"Up to you Gloria, he said he didn't want to go. I think he's okay. I hit him, yes okay I did that and he fell out of the van but honestly he's looking better all the time."

"So, you hit him, and left him in that awful warehouse place. God, I can't believe it. I thought you were nice, I really did. I assumed that whatever you had done it was a mistake, just a momentary thing, even an accident, and all the time you were – well you are, Sandie Webb's brother. I know about you." She shook her head. "Anyway, I just want you out of here. Out and gone. If you go now without any fuss I won't report you but only because I couldn't stand the embarrassment. To think I've trusted you, I've helped you. I even came to care about you." She blushed now remembering the love-making, the moments of closeness. "What an idiot. Anyway, just go, will you? I'll look after him but you just go."

"Let me pay you, for his room." For a moment fury blazed in her eyes but then she tipped her head to one side.

"Actually, yeah why not? You put him there you should pay for him. Give me two hundred quid."

Simon pushed a hand into his back pocket and brought out his credit card. He held it towards her. "I want cash. I don't want any trace of this. Give me cash."

"Okay, I need to go down to the bank."

"Right and then when you come back you pack up and go."

He left quietly, as he pulled the door closed behind him he glanced back to see Gloria opening the guest room and peering inside.

* * *

"I've got your money." Simon tapped on the white door leading to the private accommodation. "Gloria, are you there?" It wasn't closed and so he pushed at the wood. She was inside, standing before the fireplace with a glass in her hand and swiping at her nose with a tissue. Crying had stained her cheeks red and as he watched she tried to gather herself. "Are you okay?" He knew it was a stupid question. He had whispered it expecting another tirade but she lifted her head and stared at him silently across the small space.

"I'm sorry." It was the only thing he could say. She shook her head.

"I don't know how you could do that, how anyone could do that to another person. Shit, Simon, he's just a sad, fat bloke. What harm could he ever have done you? Surely you weren't afraid of him?"

"No, no, not now I'm not. I can see what you mean, I can but you don't know. You just don't know." He waited, he hoped that maybe she would relent, ask him to explain but she took the money from his hands and put it onto the mantelpiece.

"I have some of your washing in the machine. You can come back tomorrow at half ten and take it." She turned away to stare out of the window.

Simon moved back into the hall, climbed to his room where it took him just a few minutes to pack his bag. She didn't come to watch him leave.

There was no other practical option, so he walked back the way they had driven just a couple of hours ago and let himself into the warehouse. He locked the door and clambered up the uncarpeted stairs to the dilapidated living area. He glanced around, there was the kettle he had bought for while he had been working here, there was a mug and a glass and an old moth-eaten armchair that had been left behind by the last tenants. So, this was his world now. He felt that maybe it was exactly what he deserved.

Chapter 23

He wasn't homeless. He had paid the rent for this place. For the next twelve months he could stay here and do nothing more with it.

Simon spent a cold and miserable night in the scruffy, damp armchair. He was sore and cold and hungry. He may not be homeless but he certainly felt as though he was.

In order to rent the property, the owner had been obliged to keep the gas appliances maintained and certificated and so there was hot water from the old boiler. The heating should have been working but wasn't. He had slumped in the chair, wrapped one of the charity shop blankets around himself and lost his thoughts in a bottle of whisky.

Now though, he would have a look, see if he could work out what was going on with the radiators.

The nasty bathroom was cold, damp and smelled of mould. That first shower in the Bed and Breakfast had seemed like luxury after the communal nightmares of jail. Now, as he washed himself, shivering at the cracked basin that other clean and fragrant space felt like something remembered from a dream.

He dragged on his clothes then walked to the greasy spoon around the corner and ordered a full English fry up. The cold rain was back, and nursing a mug of builder's tea he watched condensation sliding down the windows to pool on the sills.

There were things he had to do and there were things he wanted to do and they were jumbled and lost in the hopeless depression that had swept in with the morning. He was trapped inside a grey plastic shroud, the rest of the world was buzzing around him, he knew that, he was aware of the noise and the scents but he was closed off, insulated and untouchable.

When the plate of bacon and eggs, beans and fried bread slammed onto the Formica in front of him he felt bile rise in his throat and had to fight to hold back the nausea.

"Something wrong love?" The waitress was middle-aged and curvy. She wore a blue overall and leaned forward breathing stale cigarette smoke at him and it was too much. He jumped up, threw a tenner on the table and stormed from the little café to fly into the alleyway at the side where he heaved up nothing more than liquid and bile.

When he stood and turned back to the road, the waitress was standing in the doorway. "You alright lad?"

"Yeah, yeah – I'm okay. Heavy night."

"Well you should come back in – eat your breakfast, get something inside you. That'll see you right."

"No, no it's fine thanks. Did I leave enough?"

"Yeah, too much, do you want your change?"

"No, keep it. Thanks." And she was gone.

He went back to the shop and let himself in by the back door. The smell of urine had lessened but in his present state it turned his stomach. He ran hot water into an old plastic bin and sluiced the floor, brushing the stained water out in to the yard.

He picked up the shackles and chains, shook them once, made them clank and jangle. He held them at arm's length. Beside the one that had been used on Hardcastle the other two were looped onto hooks he had drilled into the walls. It had all been so clear. They would have been held captive until they admitted the truth and he would have left them, chained and helpless to slowly starve or die of thirst. Afraid, helpless and imprisoned. Snarling at each other like the animals he believed they were. It was suitable justice for the fear Sandie had suffered and the years of captivity they had left him to.

He had failed at the first hurdle. When it came down to it, he hadn't had the guts for torture and killing. He was soft.

Now what?

Now that he had let his one-time friend go it was over. He would tell the others. Jason Parr and Robert Parker would soon know all about it. Would they laugh? Mock him and his failure, would they report him? It wasn't impossible. Stephen Hardcastle could be at the police station even now. Shit, he could be back in prison before the day was out. Or would they come for him? Would they decide that he was too dangerous to be allowed to roam around town?

That would be best, if they came – if they came right now he would take them on. A fair fight, well he would be outnumbered but as fair as it needed to be and when it was over he would have the truth or they would kill him.

Yes, that would be best.

Chris had changed his appointment time again, so it seemed that although he had to stick to the schedule it didn't work the other way. The note, pushed under his door back in Mill Lodge had irritated him. A message from Chris it had said. No explanation just a new day, new time and reference to his appointment. Maybe it was meant to be, earlier than planned but now it seemed that maybe he could go and not come back. Just move on – Manchester,

Liverpool anywhere to be anonymous – and he could start again.

He would go and see the graves again, Sandie and his mum. He would say goodbye, let them know that he had failed them and then disappear and take whatever came his way.

Or.

There was always the other option. There was another way to finish things, the ultimate end and maybe that would be the most honourable now – to simply finish his worthless existence here in this stinking place and leave it to others to clear away his remains if and when they found him.

Chapter 24

Because it was too hard to think of anything else, he caught the bus to Leeds. To not do it might mean police at Gloria's door and she didn't deserve that.

The day was wet and grey and he sat with his eyes closed listening to the swish of tyres on wet tarmac. He dozed a little, his head jerking upwards every time the bus pulled into a stop or swung too quickly around the corners.

The probation office reception was muggy and warm and he slouched on the uncomfortable chair feigning sleep. It was too hard to bother seeing, too hard to risk having to acknowledge anyone else.

Chris Bradbury stuck his head out of his office door. "Hello Simon. You made it then? Come on in."

He trailed across the grey carpet and, heaving a sigh, lowered himself to the wooden chair as Chris slid back behind his desk and dragged the file folder towards him.

"So, how's things?"

"Yeah, fine."

"You can't go cancelling meetings, Simon. I was able to fit you in this time but we have schedules you know. Don't do that again – right?"

He couldn't even dredge up an answer for the fussy middle aged bloke sitting opposite to him. He nodded and folded his arms across his chest.

"You don't look too good. Is there a problem?"

Simon shook his head. He would have to speak, it seemed impossibly difficult. "No, it's fine. Everything is fine. I guess I'm just tired."

"Okay. You're not hungover, are you? You need to avoid getting drunk. You know that don't you. You have to avoid anything that might lead to you losing control."

"No, not hungover. Like I said, just tired."

"Have you signed on yet?"

He felt anger begin to build but fought it back. He just wanted to get out of the place, he just wanted to be on his own. He just wanted to curl into a ball and cease to exist, without any effort or thought, he just wanted to not be there anymore, not be anywhere. Tears prickled at the back of his eyes and he had to cough to relieve the lump in his throat.

With the disintegration of his plan, life had ceased to have any meaning. There was no point signing on, no point looking for work, no point trailing back to the nasty little shop. No point to any of it. Still he had to put on a front.

"Honestly, Chris, I will. But I think I just want another couple of weeks. I'm okay for money at the moment and I would rather not draw benefit if I don't have to."

"Oh well, don't leave it until you've got nothing left."

Too late mate.

"Are you still staying at the Bed and Breakfast, what is it erm…" he riffled through the papers.

"Mill Lodge. Yeah, still there." He was safe in the knowledge that there was no way Chris could be arsed to check up, it didn't matter what he said here, it was all just paperwork.

They sat for a minute looking at each other across the cheap desk until Bradbury shrugged his shoulders, signed his name at the bottom of a page and folded the file closed. "Well, if there's nothing you want to talk to me about, no problems – questions, we can call that it." He glanced at his watch. "If you're quick you'll catch the four o'clock bus." He held out his hand.

Simon looked at it for a moment and then reached across and briefly returned the weak grip and drew back, sticking his hands into the pockets of his jeans.

Chris was already moving towards the door when he spoke again, "Same time in two weeks then. Simon, if there are any problems in the meantime you have my number." He was frowning now and made direct eye contact, looking for a brief moment as though he might be bothered to care.

It was too much and Simon shook his head, lowered his gaze and strode through the door. He needed to be outside, away from other people. He didn't want eye contact and words of concern, he wanted oblivion.

There were two chemists in the town centre and he called in both of them. There were two small supermarkets and a shop that seemed to sell something of everything, even sandwiches. By the time he walked back to the bus stop he had a carrier holding several boxes of paracetamol and a bottle of whisky. He had bought a bottle of water and sat in the back of the bus as it curled and wove its way back through the dripping countryside. He sipped at the warming liquid and allowed the thrum of the motor and the indistinct murmur of the other passengers wash over him, lulling him. When it stopped at the top end of town, near the church he climbed out and trudged through the drizzle towards the graveyard, his head down partly because of the rain blowing in his face and because it was just too much effort to hold it up anymore.

The church door was open, a yellow light shining from inside and he could hear the sound of someone vacuuming. He had never thought of it before, that a church would need to be vacuumed and the droning, homely sound made him feel even more alone.

The corner where the graves were was dark and soaked, rain dripping constantly from the huge tree, but it didn't matter. He lowered to the ground, took out the bottle of whisky, laid his head back against the trunk, closed his eyes and took a couple of huge swigs. It burned in the back of this throat and set his empty stomach on fire. Without opening his eyes, he rooted in the plastic bag and tore open the first of the packets of pills.

Chapter 25

"So here we are Sandie. I screwed up." He took another big gulp of the whisky and followed it with eight paracetamols, the whole of one little bubble pack, a small handful. They stuck in his throat and began to dissolve, he gulped more of the malt to wash them down.

He choked and coughed, and lifted his face to the cool wash of drizzle. He pulled the sleeve of his sweater down over his hand and rubbed it across his face, dried the moisture.

"Yeah, what was I saying? Oh right, well. It was going okay. I'd got that fat pig Hardcastle, squealing and crying." The alcohol on an empty stomach was working on his nerves now and he giggled, the sound surprising him and bringing his hand up to press against this mouth.

"It wasn't funny, sorry Sandie, it really wasn't funny. I belted him with a hammer. I chained him to the wall. It was just what I planned and I felt *up* you know, I felt excited. It was happening, after all the years it was happening. Oh shit." He leaned forward now, resting his forehead on his bent knees. His hair was dripping, his jeans soaked. He was dizzy from lack of sleep and alcohol.

"I thought I could do it Sandie, I wanted to so badly. For you, yes, a bit for me, for all the years wasted but mostly I wanted to do it for you. I wanted to make them pay for their part in it... shit, shit. I wanted them scared and sorry and knowing they were going to die. I was so sure, so bloody pleased with myself and then, when I woke up. When I thought of him bleeding and hurting, maybe even dying I just knew I couldn't keep on. I couldn't kill him and I couldn't kill the others and I let you down and I failed you and I'm so bloody sorry." Without raising his head, he fumbled in the plastic bag, picked out the opened box of pills. The dark behind his eyelids was comforting but he wanted to smother the overload of emotion, the whirl of drunkenness.

A touch on his arm, very gentle, tentative. At first it didn't register and she didn't speak. Knowledge that someone else was there seeped in through the anguish and he raised his head to find Gloria crouched beside him her hand resting on his arm and a large bunch of flowers on the ground beside her.

"What are you doing?" She leaned a hand against the trunk of the oak to steady herself. She didn't say any more, her eyes were steady on his.

"Why are you here?" He had no answer that he could give her and so he had responded with a question of his own. "Oh, your husband."

"God no, he was cremated, none of this planting in the cold ground for us, well for me. I think it's barbaric."

"Why then?"

"To come here. To come to Sandie's grave."

"You didn't know her. Why?"

"Because I wanted to see, where she was. Oh I don't know, something stupid about wanting to reach back, to know more. Stephen told me that she was up here and I just had this urge. Well..." She stood and lifted the bunch of flowers, laying them gently on the gravel inside the tiny wall and then stepping back just for a moment to stare in silence at the headstone.

Simon had lowered his head again, he was nauseous, soaked through and wanted her to go away and leave him alone and let him get on with what he had come here to do.

"It was nice of you to bring flowers, Gloria."

"Well, it's what you do. But you, you didn't bring flowers. What are you doing?"

"I just needed to be here that's all."

"Getting drunk in the rain next to your sister's grave. What is it Simon, guilt, regret?"

He tilted his head back now to look up at her. "I wasn't able to come when they buried her. They wouldn't let me. I came the day I got back and today I just wanted to be with her. Her and my mum."

"Why did you do it, Simon? I mean how could you do what you did? It just doesn't bear thinking about. Your own sister."

He sighed now and shook his head. He didn't have the strength for this. "I didn't, I just didn't. I loved her, I looked after her. She was my little sister. The only thing I did wrong that night was to get bored and angry waiting for her and to go off and have a walk. If I'd met her the way I was supposed to then she'd be here now."

"Yeah, you would say that, wouldn't you? But, I mean after all this time, after doing your time – maybe it would do you good to admit it and get it off your chest. It won't make any difference to anything will it – except that you'd be taking responsibility."

"Why don't you just go away, Gloria? Why don't you take your words of advice and your bracing thoughts and just go back home?"

She glared down at him and he thought for a moment she was going to kick him. Then, she stopped, bent closer and reached out to pick up the plastic carrier. He tried to grab it before she did but his hands flailed in empty air.

"Oh, I see." She twisted the handles of the bag together and folded it into her handbag. "Oh I don't think so, no." She reached out again and snatched the box of pills from where he was trying to hide them in his fist. "No, you're not doing that. You coward. You bloody coward. Get up, come on – bring your bottle if you must but get yourself up."

She grabbed him by the sleeve of his coat and forced him to his feet, he heard the fabric rip.

"Shit, you ripped it."

"Yeah well, it's only a jacket and I gave it to you anyway. Come on, come on with me."

"What? Why? No, just sod off and leave me alone."

"No, you're not doing that. You're not going to make me feel guilty. This isn't for you; this is for me. I know what it's like to grieve, to wonder if you could have done anything, to be tormented with doubt. You're not the only one who's dealt with that stuff and you're not going to do that to me. Now get yourself sorted and get in the car."

She had parked in the tiny gravelled space next to the churchyard wall and as they had spoken she forced him forward and now pushed him into the passenger seat.

"Bloody hell, my place is going to be like a sodding nursing home if this carries on. Put your seatbelt on Simon." And as he struggled with cold, numb fingers to slot the buckle together she did a rapid three-point turn and shot from the entrance, out into the main road and down towards the town.

Chapter 26

"Is he still there, at your place?" Simon slumped in the seat, his head back, eyes closed. His words were not slurred but the low, toneless delivery caused Gloria to glance across at him. She nudged him.

"Don't you fall asleep on me. If you're talking about Stephen, yes he's still there."

"Is he okay?"

"I reckon so, yes. He slept a lot but he hasn't been sick for a while and he's got up a couple of times and had something to eat. He's sore and bruised and doesn't look that pretty, but no permanent damage." She gave a huff of a laugh. "To be honest I think he's putting some of it on. He's enjoying the attention. I'll give him a day or so and then see what I can do about moving him out. Course I have no idea about mentally, what you might have done to his head. But I reckon he's okay."

"I'm glad."

"Are you? Are you really?"

He didn't speak but she was aware that he was nodding.

"Don't go to sleep," she leaned over and slapped at his leg. "How many of those pills have you taken?"

"Not many, not many at all."

"Okay, but how many?"

"Oh, only one lot, one sheet of them."

"Oh right, well that's probably about eight or twelve, is it?"

"Dunno – I reckon."

"Well, that's good. You might be okay. You are drunk though, aren't you?"

"I'm tired, really tired and I haven't eaten anything and then I had the whisky." He lifted the bottle and shook it in front of his face. There was a small amount left in the bottom. "Huh, more than I thought. Yeah I guess I might be a bit drunk."

She turned into the parking place in front of her hotel. "Can you manage on your own?"

"Yes, yes, I reckon. Gloria, I think it's best if I just go. You couldn't just take me up to the shop, could you? I'll be okay if you just take me up there."

"No bloody way. I don't trust you and there's no way I'm going to be sitting here in a week wishing I'd done more. No, you'll come in and have some coffee and then we'll see." She leaned over now and opened the door for him. "Go on, we'll use the front door. I've got a couple of guests, proper ones, you know the sort that pay me! So, keep the noise down."

Once they were inside she steered him into her private rooms and pointed at the sofa and then grabbed his arm. Your trousers are filthy, just a minute." She went to the bedroom and brought him her husband's dressing gown and a towel. "Dry your hair and then sit down. Leave your clothes in the corner, I'll stick them in the dryer."

In the warm room, dry now and calmer Simon was overwhelmed with sadness. He leaned back against the cushions and closed his eyes.

The smell of coffee and bread toasting wafted through from the kitchen and he could hear Gloria clattering about with cups and plates.

"I'm sorry."

"What, I can't hear you, just a sec."

He stood and staggered across the room.

"I said I'm sorry. You don't deserve all this Gloria. You're a good person and you shouldn't be having to do this. Look let me go and I promise I won't do – well – what I was going to do. I won't do that to you."

She had turned now to look at him. "Go and sit down. Just go and sit on the couch. We'll have a drink. We'll talk and see what's best."

He forced down the toast while Gloria sat beside the fire nursing her mug of coffee. They didn't speak until he put the plate back onto the tray and picked up his own drink.

"You can't carry on like this, can you?" She turned now and looked at him. "I mean, you've done your time. Paid for what you did and you have to just carry on now. You have to try and make some sort of life for yourself, don't you? Let the past stay where it belongs."

Before she had finished speaking he slapped the mug back onto the table. "Gloria, I can't. I can't move on – there is no 'on' for me. I have spent over fifteen years with this. The guilt..."

She turned towards him quickly and he held up his hand.

"No, not that, not guilt about that. Guilt because I let it happen, I let her down, it was my fault but I didn't do anything to her. I would never have hurt her. She was my little sister, I remember her being born, the first time they let me hold her. I could never have hurt her. I didn't do it."

"But you were found guilty. I looked it up online. When I knew who you were – are."

"Yes."

"That doesn't happen though, not really. Innocent people going to jail. They must have been convinced, the jury, the judge. They found you guilty."

"I know. I was framed, well maybe that's not the right word. I don't know but I was a scapegoat. The evidence was circumstantial, my sweater in the ditch near where they found her, the fact that nobody saw me out on the moor. The cigarette ends near where she'd been. But, I didn't do it. I just didn't."

Gloria put down her mug, she didn't speak but twisted in her seat and looked straight at him, the invitation was in her eyes, she nodded and he began to talk, to tell her what they had done to him.

Chapter 27

She didn't interrupt, didn't ask questions or make any comments. Now and then she would nod but mostly she sat comfortably in her chair and listened.

Then he had finished. Told her everything from the break-up with Tracey to the moment the judge had given his sentence and they took him away, amid shouts and jeers and that look, that last blank look from his father.

Afterwards, as he finished speaking and gave a shrug of his shoulders before leaning back against the cushion, they sat in silence. There was just the clicking of things cooling, the quiet sound of footsteps in one of the guests' rooms upstairs and the occasional rumble of a bus or a lorry on the road outside.

He waited, expecting a judgement, a declaration of disbelief or maybe an empty comment about the unfairness of it.

After a couple of minutes, she got up, put the cups and plates together on the tray and turned towards the kitchen. "I'll run you up to the shop later, you can collect your things. Your old room is still vacant so you won't need to move into another one."

She left him speechless.

* * *

"I think when you have a minute you should take that stuff down. It looks odd and, to be honest we don't know what Stephen is going to do." Gloria had paused for a moment on her way through the workshop towards the flat and waved a hand at the chains and rings in the wall. Three of them, carefully positioned and hefty.

"Yeah. I will." He had noticed her use of the word 'we', it didn't seem possible that, after all this time, he had someone on his side. He wasn't sure how to deal with it.

"We've got this place for a year, unless we can sub-let which frankly I think is pretty much impossible. What are you going to do with it?"

"How do you mean?"

"Well, I was thinking that I could give you a hand. When I have time, you know, maybe you could make it nice enough to move into. Seeing as you've paid the rent anyway."

"Oh yeah, right of course. You need your room back. I'll move out as soon as I can."

"Well, it wasn't that so much, to be honest at the moment I'm glad of the money but later on my prices should go up." She shook her head, "no you've taken me down the wrong road. That wasn't what I was thinking. It's just that if you have an address, a proper one, it's a start isn't it. A start to move on, for afterwards."

"Afterwards?"

"Yes, for when you've settled all this other stuff. You'll need somewhere to live won't you, and what about the business, the printing thing?"

"Oh well, that. I... erm... okay, cards on the table – that was a lie."

She nodded at him.

"I just needed to get this place. It wasn't all baloney. I did do the extra courses while I was in jail and I do know

112

about printing. It's what I did before, I did quite a few courses. It passes the time, keeps your head together."

"Well there we are then."

"No, no, it was just part of the plan."

"The only part that made any sense if you ask me. But you know, you could give it a go, couldn't you? I was convinced when you told me about it. Anyway, that's for later, I mean. I know there's other stuff to deal with first, but after."

He turned in a small circle. "I suppose I could do the flat anyway and then think about the rest of it."

He laughed and Gloria tipped a head to one side, looked at him quizzically.

"What?"

"Well, it's just that I've never had a place of my own. It's only just occurred to me. I was at my mum and dad's before and then – well you know."

"Hmm – not ideal is it, but you've got it so you might as well do something with it. What will you do about your dad? Are you giving up on that now?"

"Yeah, I think so for now at least. Maybe later, if any of this ever gets sorted, well maybe there could be a chance."

"Right, come on. I've got stuff to do we can't stand around here gassing all day and you look bloody awful. I reckon you need to have a proper meal and then get to bed." She stormed past him now carrying one of the bags.

"Gloria."

"Oh, what now?"

"Well, just, thanks."

She smiled and nodded at him and then turned to clatter down the stairs and back out to the yard where she flung his bag into her car and climbed inside to wait for him. She had moved quickly so that he hadn't had the chance to see the moisture in her eyes. She could be making a monumental mistake and regret may be just around the corner but she didn't think so and if the story

113

he told her was true then there was a wrong here that must be put right.

Back at the hotel she left Simon to settle back in the room while she prepared some food for them and for Hardcastle. He was probably well enough to go home now but they would keep him here just a little longer, until they knew he wasn't going to cause them any trouble, and they really needed to talk to him.

Chapter 28

"I made you some sausage, mash and onion gravy." Gloria could tell by the look on his face that she had judged her overweight guest's preferences spot on. It was the first proper meal she had made for him, he had eaten soup and scrambled eggs with no complaint but it was time to make him believe he was recovering. "I brought you a glass of beer. I reckon you'll be okay now to have a drink. I'll put them on the little table. Enjoy." She left, thanking the gods of ready meals and didn't bother to worry about the teeny lie, she had heated and served it after all. He spoke, halting her at the door.

"Have you had your tea?"

"No, not yet."

"I thought maybe we could eat together," he grinned at her.

"Well, I make it a rule not to eat with the guests, Stephen, try to keep things professional you know."

His face fell and he pouted with disappointment but he got the message. She needed to keep him sweet but not to the extent that he started flirting with her. She shuddered at the thought of the sweaty, greasy bulk of him anywhere near her.

Simon was waiting in her rooms with a glass of wine. There was a strangeness between them, as if they had just met.

"How is he?"

"Flirting!" As she said it she gave an exaggerated shudder followed by a little giggle.

"Oh god! Does he know I'm back?"

"I haven't said anything. It needs some thinking about, doesn't it? He's probably the first step so we need to make it work. We need a plan."

"I had a plan, look where that got me."

"Yes. I know. What we need now though is a plan that won't involve breaking the law – well not much if we can help it anyway – and you coming out clean at the end of it."

They ate together and talked well into the night. Simon wasn't sure just how far the new closeness would go, just what the recent events had done to their relationship. In her own way, Gloria dealt with the situation in just one moment. Did you turn your radiator on? I turn them off in the vacant rooms so it might be a bit chilly."

"Right. No, I didn't. I'll go and do that. Perhaps I'll have a shower. Then tomorrow in the morning we'll see how far we get with Stevo."

"Yeah, great." She held out her hand for his empty glass and then as he moved towards the door she went through to the kitchen. "Night Simon. Sleep well. We'll make this work, just you wait."

Before he climbed the stairs, Simon stopped to listen outside Hardcastle's door. He heard the rattling snores.

He didn't know how to feel now. On the one hand, he had a friend, who believed him and wanted to help. On the other hand, his chilly room was lonely when he knew that Gloria would be snuggling down under her feather duvet. He regretted the loss of their closeness. He had failed in his plan but more than that it had cost him something precious.

She for her part stood at the back door looking out to the dark moor, another glass of whisky in her hand, her mind alive with scurrying thoughts, doubts and worries. She had committed to this now and she would see it through to the end, but her hand shook as she lifted the glass to her lips and her mouth was dry with apprehension.

An owl called to the darkness and the haunting, lonely sound drove her back inside. She walked to the sideboard and picked up the picture of her husband. She studied it for a moment and then replaced it on the shining surface. The circles of life were twined and connected but when she took the booking all those weeks ago, she could not have known just where this particular spiral was going to lead.

Her other guests had returned so, with a quick check of the locks at the front door, she went through to get ready for bed.

Out there in the cold a teenage girl lay under the cold ground and what of the people who were responsible for that, what of those who thought this thing had gone away? How would they react when it came back to them?

This was frightening, it was nasty and she hadn't asked for it. All she had done was take the booking for a room but now – she was in it and she knew she would stick until the truth was known, whatever that might be.

Chapter 29

Simon knocked on the door.

"Come in love." Hardcastle stepped out of the shower room with a towel almost covering his belly. He had known that Gloria usually brought his breakfast at this time. "Oh, it's you. What are you doin' bringing trays round? You don't work here, do you?"

"No, but Gloria is a friend, I was helping her. Just as well, eh, wouldn't want her to catch sight of that." He nodded his head in the direction of the gap where the towel didn't meet. The other man grabbed the edges of the cloth and tried to drag them closer around himself.

"Still trying to pull the birds then?"

"Don't be bloody daft. I heard your voice. I knew it wasn't Gloria."

"Yeah, that why you called me love, was it?" Simon put the tray onto a small table set before the window. "There's your breakfast anyway. When you've had that, we need to talk."

"I haven't got anything to say to you. I'm not going to sit down with you anywhere. I might still go to the cops anyroad. That Gloria asked me not to but I dunno. What you did, that were right out of order. I nearly died."

Simon turned at the door and stared across the room at the half naked man. As the silence grew Hardcastle blushed and fidgeted. "Bugger off anyroad. I want to get dressed. I'm getting cold."

Simon plucked a dressing gown from the edge of the bed and tossed it across the room. As he grabbed out at it the towel fell to the floor leaving the fat body exposed and Hardcastle flustered.

"We're talking later. Enjoy your bacon." As he stepped into the hall Simon turned the key in the lock. He was sure that the thought of security hadn't crossed the other man's mind and now he made a point of rattling the door handle, driving home the point that there was no way out. Yes, there was a window but all the ground floor rooms had extra security and anyway the fat bulk of Hardcastle wouldn't fit through.

Gloria was crossing on her way from the dining room and she raised her eyebrows. Simon nodded at her and then followed her into the kitchen.

"Is he okay?"

"Yeah, puffing and blowing but I reckon he's fine. Thanks to you, Gloria, when I think about how close I came to killing him it makes me feel sick. It's funny, all the time I was thinking about it, planning it I don't think I ever really appreciated what it would mean. You pulled me back from the brink."

"No, you'd already done that."

"Well maybe, but you made sure. You helped me when all you needed to do was turn away."

"Bloody hell, I couldn't have done that – turn away and let you kill someone. No, that was never an option. Anyway, we're moving on, that's gone – done and dusted. I don't really want him in my space so I think we'll take him into the dining room when all the guests have gone out. They won't be long I don't think."

"Come in Stephen. I made some coffee and there's a couple of scones."

"Aw thanks love." He lowered himself carefully onto the dining chair and glanced around. "It's nice this. I could eat in here next."

"Ah well. That's one of the things I need to talk to you about. I was thinking that you are probably well enough to go home now, don't you?" Gloria had never seen such a visible demonstration of the saying 'his face fell'. Indeed, the flabby cheeks and fat jowls did visibly seem to drop.

"Oh, well I don't know – I've still got all these bruises." He lifted his shirt to expose the yellowing marks on his skin.

"Yes, I know and actually I wasn't thinking that you would have to look after yourself completely. I know it must still be difficult for you. I wondered if you would like to pop in for your breakfast for a day or two. Just until you're completely back on your feet. Only I need the room. I have someone coming who uses a wheelchair and I only have one disabled one."

"I could move upstairs."

She smiled at him and leaned over to pat his hand, offered him another scone and watched as he loaded it with butter and jam.

"I haven't got any vacancies I'm afraid."

"Well I wouldn't have thought you'd be that busy, not this time of the year."

"No, it's great isn't it." She could tell he was unconvinced.

"I don't know. I'm not sure as 'ow I can manage. I might have to go up the hospital."

She felt her blood begin to boil. "Well, that's up to you, I suppose. I can run you up there if you like. Of course they are going to wonder why you left it so long. I expect when you explain they'll want to call the police as well but if you think that's what you want." She shrugged her shoulders.

"Ah well, breakfast you say."

"Just until next week. I suppose you'll be wanting to get back to work by then."

He knew he had lost and so took what he could. "Aye, well alright then. Will you give me a lift home?"

"Of course I will. Before we do that though Stephen, Simon wants a word with you. I'll just go and get him." She ignored the look of fear on his face and called through to the kitchen. "Simon – are you there?"

* * *

"I'm not tellin' you nowt – let's understand that up front. Nowt – more than my life's worth, so you can give up on that idea right now."

Simon sat across the table and stared into eyes that flicked and darted nervously about. He watched as the other man took in the scar and the unflinching gaze. "I think you will. No matter what you think other people might do to you, I can do worse. I've served my time and I've paid my dues and now it's time to collect." He ran his finger along the puckered pale skin that ran across his cheek. The message was clear but he drove it home. "No matter how hard you think you are, how hard your mates are – I can assure you I've met harder and beaten them. Now where shall we start?"

Chapter 30

No matter how scared he was, how much Simon threatened – towering over Hardcastle who sat, head lowered now, staring at the scone crumbs – they couldn't make him speak out. "I know you were in on it. I know you have the names. If you tell me whose idea it was, we'll leave it at that. Or was it you that hurt Sandie?" This was the only time they had a proper reaction. He pulled out a grubby handkerchief and mopped at his face.

"I never touched her. I never would have. She was no more than a kid. I never touched her. I'd known her forever, she was like my sister." And that was it, all he would say. No matter how intimidating he found Simon, there was someone else much more frightening, somewhere.

Gloria helped him pack the few things she had brought to him from his house a couple of days before and then ferried him home. She called in the supermarket to buy some milk, beer and a couple of ready meals and took them back to the little terraced house. Hardcastle sat in the armchair in front of the gas fire and she perched on the edge of the sofa.

"You know don't you Stephen? You know who hurt Sandie, what happened that night and why. You know who told the lies. It must have eaten away at you all these years. Knowing that the wrong man was in jail."

"'Ow do you know that, eh? You know nowt about any of it. You're just an incomer, Leeds, wasn't it? You weren't here so I don't know why you think it's any of your business. If you've got the hots for him, that Simon, Tommy, whatever he calls himself, tell him to leave it be. He's done his time now, tell him to just move on. No good can come of any of this."

She shrugged. "You're not going to tell anyone, are you?"

"How d'ya mean?"

"Well you know, about the warehouse. You peeing in your pants and everything." She knew that if she concentrated on the shame and embarrassment his male pride would be their friend. But he wasn't going to let her have it all her own way. Back in his own home with Simon far away some of his bravado returned.

"Ah well, I haven't made my mind up, have I? I could have him put away again." He nodded his head.

"Yes you could, I suppose, but then everyone would know how easily he took you, what happened with," she pointed at his trousers, "I don't think that would be much fun, and it would never be over."

"How d'ya mean?"

"Well when he came out again he would have another grudge against you, wouldn't he? You would always be looking over your shoulder, nervous in the back alleys. You with your late shifts and so on."

"Oh go on, bugger off – get back to your fancy man. I'll be in for my breakfast tomorrow mind, the full works."

She left him, there was nothing further she could do.

As she pulled out into the traffic and turned towards home Hardcastle watched her from the window. He picked up the handset of the grey plastic phone on the window sill. He began to dial then lifted his fingers to his face and gently touched his healing nose. He shook his head, replaced the receiver and then went online. He logged on to his favourite travel site. He didn't have much money in the bank but there was enough if he was careful. He'd make a booking now and sort out the fine details later. Shame about the breakfasts, he'd go tomorrow but then he'd be away. He'd have to ask the woman next door to water his plants but he didn't want to see her with his face black and blue. He'd leave a note. He rang the bus garage.

"Hello Moira, it's me Steve Hardcastle. Oh yeah, I'm gettin' better thanks. That's why I rang though. I went to the doc and he thinks I need a break. I didn't want to go on the sick so I'll take my holiday. I've got plenty accrued." He had expected the tut and the sigh, it didn't bother him, this part was easy. "I know it's a bit inconvenient but will ya take me off the schedule for the next three weeks? Yeah. Three weeks. Ta."

Three weeks, what would he do if it wasn't long enough? How would he know if it had been sorted? He picked the phone up again. "Robert. It's Stevo. No, I'm not so good mate. I'm goin' away for a bit. If you can manage it I think you should as well, or at least keep your head down. That Tommy's on the rampage. Got the bit between his teeth sommat shocking. I'll call you in a day or so, you won't believe what he did. Take care mate, eh? I'll see you when I see you. I'll give you a buzz, keep in touch."

He climbed wearily up the stairs to sort out clothes for his trip. He lowered himself onto the end of his bed and closed his eyes and then, with a grunt, he stood up and dragged open his wardrobe.

* * *

Gloria stood in the doorway of her little kitchen, Simon was making them coffee. "Did he tell you anything?"

"No, I tried but there was no moving him at all. Whatever he knows, and he knows something of course, whatever it is, he's keeping his mouth shut. What next Simon?"

"I thought I might have a go at Robert but then, why? Why mess about, the one I should be dealing with is bloody Jason Parr. He was always the leader, I was scared of him, just as much as they were."

"If you were scared of him, why did you hang around with him? That's daft."

"Yeah, well, being with him we felt like the big guys. He swaggered and we swaggered with him. People got out of his way and so they got out of our way as well. He was a wheeler and dealer, into everything dodgy."

"But you weren't like them were you. You had a job, a home and family."

"Yeah, well I was bored and he was the most exciting thing around. I was stupid, but I was young and you're supposed to be stupid when you're young and get away with it aren't you? Only I didn't, me and Sandie didn't."

"Okay then, Jason Parr it is." Gloria swallowed the lump of fear that rose as she spoke.

Chapter 31

"Tell me about her. If it's too hard I understand but if you can, tell me about Sandie. Not just about that night, tell me about her."

Simon shifted in his chair, took a sip of whisky. "She was special. I know lots of people think that about their sister, brother whatever, you should do, shouldn't you? But she was. She was very pretty, well at fourteen most girls are, aren't they? Unless they're really unlucky, I suppose. But with Sandie it was more, she was so fit, strong and healthy, she used to glow with it. She was a runner; bloody fast she was. They reckoned that she could have gone all the way to the top, even to the Olympics. Her P.E. teacher said that she was outstanding and she started running for the county when she was only thirteen and a half. Running and winning, always winning. She was amazing to watch. You know when you see these joggers staggering around, looking all awkward and pained…"

Gloria laughed and nodded.

"Well she looked nothing like that, she looked so good, as if she was almost flying. Everything just right. Of course, when she finished, she was out of breath and in pain. I didn't know until Sandie that it's so painful, doing something like that. You have to really, really want to do it because it's easier not to and that was it, she lived for it. She trained every day, at school and at the sports centre. I used to meet her on my way home from work, wait for her and then walk her home."

"I remember my mum having her and then when she came home from the hospital and they let me hold her. I was scared stiff, she was so small and I thought I'd hurt her. Then I remember the first time she smiled at me – God…" He was overcome and Gloria came to his rescue.

"So, running that's where she'd been. The night she went missing. I read it in the reports online."

"Yes, she was late but sometimes she would do some extra or get talking with her coach. It wasn't that unusual and normally it didn't matter. She'd come out all excited and tell me about it, her times and that. But that night," he stopped again and took in a deep breath. "Well I was mad. Tracey had come to work at lunch time and said she wanted to finish with me. She was fed up with me going out with my mates nearly every night. She never liked them, especially not Jason, so she wouldn't come. Usually I'd go and see her for an hour and then meet the others in the pub. Anyway, she said she'd had enough. If I wanted to be with them more than her she wasn't having it. So, I was angry and confused I suppose, because I didn't know whether I really did – want to be with them more. Thing was though, I knew if I told them I was going to spend more time with her they'd never let me hear the back of it. God, this is all so stupid now."

"It probably didn't seem like it at the time though. What were you, nineteen?"

"I was just going on twenty. Anyway, I did go and wait for Sandie for a bit but she was late and I was frustrated and in the end I just thought – sod it. It wasn't dark, the light was going but it wasn't dark and it was a lovely evening so I just walked up the road, past the church and out onto the moor. I stomped about for an hour or so, and then I went home."

"And that's when you found out she hadn't arrived."

"Yeah, like I told you the other day, my dad was steaming. He was mad with her for not coming home and he was mad with me for not waiting for her. Anyway, we went out and walked around. The sports centre was all closed up. We went to her mates' houses, she didn't have that many, always too busy training. We walked all over town but she wasn't anywhere and by now it was dark. When it got to half eleven my dad rang the police and that was when it all fell in on us."

Gloria went to kneel beside him. "I am so sorry Simon, I don't think I've said that to you before. It must have been horrible, and all made worse because of what happened afterwards. I understand your bitterness. Stephen said something though, he said why don't you just let it go?" She stopped and looked at him, saw his face harden and the knuckles grow white as he gripped the glass tighter.

"No, no."

She leaned in and kissed him, warm and inviting. "Do you want to stay here tonight? You can if you want."

He wrapped his arms around her, burying his head into her shoulder and she felt him nod.

"We'll get on with it tomorrow. We have to get this sorted because otherwise you're never going to get yourself together, are you? Tomorrow, Simon."

Later he lay in the warm bed, Gloria sleeping with her legs wrapped around his, soft and sated from the lovemaking. It was wonderful and he knew that it could be his, all this and whatever else he chose to make of himself and it would appear to be easy. To get up in the morning and just start a new life. But it would be a world built of sand and it would have no longevity and every day would have a hole in it.

Eventually he drifted off to sleep, there were good things waiting for him, but it had to start right with the past in its place and all the debts paid.

Chapter 32

Simon went the long way round to the pub, he still couldn't find the courage to walk past his dad's house. Maybe at some stage he'd give it another go but not now. At six in the evening it was still quiet but it wouldn't be long before the regulars started to trickle in. Jack would be there; he was there every night. Since he lost his job decades ago the pub had been his second home, even before Sandie's murder he had been a fixture. Simon picked up the beer that had been poured as soon as the door opened and the old man hobbled in. He nodded at the barmaid to let her know it was his shout. As Jack settled in his usual seat beside the fireplace Simon put the glass down in front of him. "Cheers Jack." He watched the battle take place, the narrowing of the old bloke's eyes, the twitch of his shoulders. He didn't want to talk but he did want the drink. Inevitably the drink won.

"Thanks," he mumbled and as he tipped his glass in acknowledgement, just a little, Jack avoided eye contact. He stared into the fire as Simon pulled a chair up beside the table and sat down.

"So, Jack, long time since we had a natter."

"Aye."

"Not much has changed around here."

"No, not so much. What do you want, Tommy?" Obviously, the old man didn't have time for verbal fencing, he just wanted to get on with his drink and sit in peace. Simon could match his mood, it suited him fine.

"I want to know where Jason Parr drinks these days, that's all. I know he's barred from here so where does he go?"

"How should I know?"

"You'd know because you're thick with the family, Jack. You always were. His dad and you go way back. I only want to talk to him."

"Oh aye, 'course you do. What do you take me for lad?"

"Just tell me where he drinks at night, Jack, that's all. I won't let him know it was you."

"Aye, what about all these folks here. Do you not think they've seen? Do you not think they'll be formin' a line to tell him? *Oh aye – I saw Old Jack with that Tommy Webb. Bought him a drink an' all.*" As if the thought had just found purchase, the old man turned to the barmaid, called across the quiet pub, "I'll be paying for this myself." He waited until she nodded at him then turned back to grin at Simon. "Was there anything else lad?"

* * *

As Simon left the pub he heard the rumble of voices behind him. Well, that had worked, before the night was out Jason would know he was looking and it wouldn't be long before they met up – it was a given. The thug wouldn't want it thought he'd backed down, so it was only a question of time. Simon smiled, he hadn't even had to pay for the beer.

He crossed the road turned right into Bridge Street and then right again into Hope Street. He was heading to the graveyard, avoiding his old home. He was disoriented for a moment as he glanced down towards the river. The old factory that had stood on what was now a swathe of green, with stone pathways criss-crossing and a climbing frame in the middle, had been demolished. He hadn't known that from here, he would see so clearly the place where they had found her. He had intended to go to the graveyard to tell her that it was all under control that things were looking up and it was all going to be okay after all. Now, he couldn't face it and he turned at the end of the street and half jogged down Church Street into the town centre and The Oak where he ordered a pint and a whisky chaser. He hadn't been ready for that and it had winded him, and taken the buzz out of his small victory with Jack.

His nerves calmed as he walked back to Mill Lodge and the warmth of Gloria's apartment.

"You look as if you've seen a ghost. Are you okay?" Gloria asked.

"Yeah, I'm okay. I just had a bit of a shock. They knocked the old wire works down."

"Yes, two or three years ago. Made a park I think."

"Aye, that's it. I was going up to the church and it took me by surprise."

"Oh, did you used to work there?"

"No, nothing like that. It was the view. You can see all the way down to the river. You didn't used to be able to."

She shook her head, puzzled by what he was trying to tell her.

"It's the copse, that little plantation."

She still stared at him blankly.

"It was where they found her. It was more isolated then. The factory had fences round it and it wasn't very nice. Nobody went there much, but that was where she was. By the river."

"Oh god. That must have been horrible. You've never been there since?"

"No, I was arrested pretty quickly you know. Once they found my jumper and the lads dropped me in it, that was that."

132

"Simon, how do you think that happened, your jumper being there?"

"I told them over and over. Sandie used to borrow my stuff, my jumpers, sometimes even my shirts. She loved wearing clothes that were too big, especially when she'd been training. We had loads of rows about it." He smiled sadly. "Anyway, nobody believed me. They didn't find her bag, no training clothes just my jumper and the coach said she was wearing her own stuff when she left the club. With everything else it just slotted into place as one more count against me."

"I wonder what happened to her bag."

"I've always thought the murderer took it, but no matter I should think that by now it'll be long gone."

"The cigarette ends that they found, they were yours. Were they nearby when they found her?"

"No, no, they were up by the club where I'd waited to meet her. It was pathetic really, I waited there every day and of course there were fag ends, and of course they were my brand. How would there not be? I never made any pretence of the fact that I waited. The trouble was they didn't believe that I would wait and then leave and just go away. Nobody saw me on the moor and the need for the police to wind it up quickly, well... mind it was Jason and that lot who clinched it, saying they had expected me and I didn't turn up and that was unusual."

"What about DNA?"

Simon shook his head. "No, not back then."

"No, but what about now. They can do it now, can't they? She was raped wasn't she – sorry."

"Yes."

"Well I wonder if they could, you know find DNA after all this time."

"Bloody hell, do you mean from her body? Shit, no."

"Okay, okay – I know it's horrible but it could prove it wasn't you."

"No, I don't think they could find out anyway but I just wouldn't have it. No."

She nodded her head and wrapped her arms around him. "I suppose we'd never get anyone to listen anyway. As far as the law is concerned it's all cut and dried."

Chapter 33

"Have you really thought through what you're going to say to him, that Jason?" Gloria tipped her head to one side as she asked the question.

As he answered, Simon shook his head, shrugged. "Not really, I keep trying and then I get lost. I suppose I'll just wing it."

"But Simon, if he doesn't know where you're staying, how is he going to get in touch?"

Simon sighed, "Oh, he'll find me. I'm just going to walk around town tomorrow, hang about by the bookmakers. If he doesn't find me, then I guess I'll just go there. I didn't want to do that – it's sort of on his turf and I would prefer somewhere more neutral. Anyway, we'll see what happens tomorrow."

* * *

It was wet and a cold wind blew down from the moors. Simon borrowed the dead Dave Bartlett's coat and as he put it on, Gloria reached across and touched the sleeve where there was a small tear.

"You might as well just keep this you know. It fits you well and at least it's getting used." Her eyes clouded over and Simon took her into a warm hug. He didn't thank her; he didn't have the right words.

As he strode down towards the town centre he was super sensitive to the people and traffic around him. He neared the alley where Jason had confronted him before and slowed. Unlike the last time, he wanted this, a chance to speak and to make them understand that no matter how cowed they had assumed him to be, they had made a mistake. The Tommy Webb who was convicted and sent down was not the person he was now.

He spent some time walking around the main roads and then went up to the betting shop. He paused outside and peered in between the signs filling the windows. Jason wasn't there yet, so the choice was to loiter outside in the rain or go inside and spend the time watching the screen and the punters. Jason would come, he hardly ever missed a day and if not this time then there would be tomorrow.

He could go to the house of course, just hammer on the door and demand to be heard but the result of that would inevitably be physical violence and his parole would be revoked immediately. It had to be a chance encounter and any aggression must appear to come from Jason.

Simon's nerves were popping and hanging around with a bunch of elderly men eking out their pensions, filling their empty hours with vicarious thrill, was as depressing as it was boring. He left and turned back towards the town centre.

A prickle in the hairs at the back of his neck urged him to turn around, he fought the instinct. He hadn't heard anyone but was sure he was there. He glanced left and right and crossed the road, away from the terrace of houses with narrow ginnels between. He needed to keep it in the open.

From the edge of his vision he saw the flash of trainers, blue jeans. He slowed now, breathed slowly, steeled himself.

"You lookin' for me?"

"Jason."

"I said you lookin' for me? Folk keep tellin' me you're askin' after me."

Simon didn't turn – not yet. "I wanted a word, yes."

"Well here I am, have your word."

He stopped now, they were alongside the old infant school. There were shops and houses opposite but behind them just dirty stone, six feet high. "You must have known I'd come Jason. You must have known all these years that I'd come back."

"I didn't, I reckoned as how they'd get rid of you in jail. We know what happens in those places, how child killers are treated. I kept expectin' to hear that you'd been seen off."

"Well," Simon raised his hand, touched the scar across his face and then dropped it again. "Here I am. I want to ask you a few things but first of all – tell me. How did you sleep, all those years with that darkness in your mind? How did you function?"

Jason stepped close, sharp and sudden. He pushed in, forcing Simon back against the wall trying to pin him with his right arm raised, bent at the elbow, attempting to get it across Simon's throat but unable to complete the move, leaving it in the end over his chest, leaning all his weight against it.

"I slept just fine Tommy." He drew back his fist now as their feet scrabbled on the flagstones, slipping in the wet. Simon wrapped his hand around the powerful arm and dragged it away, twisting and pushing but Jason was an experienced street brawler. He moved back, changed his position and punched out with a sharp left. Simon ducked and the bare knuckles overshot and grazed against the wall. Jason hissed with the sting of it. He pivoted on his toes and came back grabbing out, aiming for shoulder, neck, head, whatever he could grab. Simon ducked, the hours in the gym in jail, the miles walking the moors and years of hate and fury were behind his arm now as he punched from the shoulder connecting with Jason's jaw, whipping his head around and knocking him off balance.

Now, to take advantage he stepped back, fists clenched, legs braced for the next assault.

He saw the glint of blade, it had been quick and he had no knife of his own. It was too great a risk to be found with anything that could be a weapon. He couldn't run though; he mustn't fail now. He raised his right leg and turned it at the knee, before Jason could react he shot the kick hard, connected with his heel against Jason's belly. The kickboxing move had been practiced against the heavy bag, never before against a soft human – he was surprised at the give in living flesh. Jason bent double and staggered back against the wall but didn't drop the knife. He gasped for breath though, and was already beginning to straighten. Simon came at him again, he didn't mess about now with finesse, he kicked out straight at Jason's groin and brought him down in a ball yelling with pain and fright on the wet pavement. Simon stomped down on his upper arm, once, twice and when Jason moved to escape the next assault, he moved his attention to his wrist. With his foot pinning the arm he bent, uncurled the fingers and pulled the knife away. He swung his leg over and knelt astride Jason's chest looking down into the watering eyes and the angry, twisted face. He pressed the blade into skin just above the black leather collar and watched terror feed into residual pain.

He had waited so long for this moment, imagined it over and over. Jason Parr at his mercy, on the blade of his knife. He could do it now, one quick move and it would be over. His hand shook with tension, his breath was short and the pounding in his chest echoed thunder in his brain.

"Hey, you – bloody well cut it out! I've called the police. Bugger off out of it, that's a school there, what the hell are you doing. Carryin' on like that where there might be kiddies." The woman was leaning from an upstairs window of one of the little houses opposite. Her voice was shrill and angry and the mention of the police spurred Simon on, he had to get away, but it wasn't over yet.

He grabbed a handful of Jason's coat and dragged him to his feet. With the knife still pressed against his neck, he forced him on down the road. The other man was staggering with pain, he gagged and vomited over his feet but still Simon moved him forward. There was a narrow pathway beside the school and with the sound of sirens growing nearer he shuffled them onwards, down towards the park where there would be cover and quiet and the chance to speak now, while he had the upper hand.

He flung Jason into the bushes beside the path, the other man was recovering quickly and so Simon sat astride him, his knees pressing the muscular upper arms into the soft soil and he leaned close. He held the sharp pointed blade of the knife inches from Jason's right eye. Jason closed the lids, squeezing them tight but fear of the unseen forced them open again.

They could hear the screech of tyres in the road and the woman shouting to the police.

Simon leaned close. "Did you hurt her, Sandie? Was it you or you and someone else?"

"Me, bloody hell. Why?"

Time was running out, he could hear the slam of car doors and pounding feet, along the top of the road and round into the small lane. "Why did you drop me in it if it wasn't you? Tell me now, convince me or I'll cut you, I'll cut your eye out. If it was you, you'll pay but if you don't tell me you'll pay harder and you'll pay now."

"Shit, of course it wasn't me. She was a kid; I'd known her forever. It wasn't me."

The knife was close now, the feet were pounding nearer and Jason was squirming and twisting. "I'm coming back for you Jason. I'm coming back and you're going to tell me everything."

"It wasn't me. I didn't do anything to her, I wasn't even there."

Simon raised up to a crouch and pushed through the undergrowth. As he ran, slipping and skidding up a sopping grassy slope he heard the police call out behind him. He rolled over the brow of the hillock and slid on his behind, pushing and thrusting with his hands and heels down towards the gravel beneath the wall. It was high but not too high, his hands slipped against the coping stones but he braced his feet against the blocks and scrambled over into the road at the other side.

He could still hear the shouts and there was a dog but he ran without looking back, dodged down a narrow snicket and over a wall into the yard space of an old car maintenance workshop.

His lungs were screaming now, his head pounding but there was no time to slow and he hurtled towards the metal gates at the entrance. They were made of vertical struts of steel with no cross pieces but secured with a heavy chain and padlock. He jumped and, on the second attempt, caught a toe hold on the chain which was just enough to boost him over the top. As he flipped over the metal bar to drop and roll on the cracked pavement he heard a quiet clink. His cheap phone was in pieces spread across the concrete on the inside of the gate. He bent and reached to try and retrieve it but the battery had skidded too far away. There was no time, he had to leave it. He glanced back towards the park and it seemed that he might have made it, might have escaped but he had to move now while there was no-one behind him. He tugged at his jacket and brushed the wet leaves and debris from his sleeves and jeans, crossed the road, sprinted down the space between two storage units and out into the main road.

There was a small café standing on the corner, he pushed through the door and into the almost deserted interior. He glanced around for a table in the back, one that hadn't been cleared since the last customer had left. There was one in the corner near to the counter, he dragged out the chair, slipped out of his jacket, picked up an abandoned newspaper and held it in front of his face. As the old man from behind the counter came across to clear and wipe the table and take his order for a pot of tea he saw the police cars cruise past.

"More bloody trouble in the park, I'll bet." The old man didn't wait for a response, and Simon's heart was juddering so rapidly that he couldn't form one anyway.

As he drank the tea and waited until he thought it would be safe to leave, he re-played the scene over and over in his mind. Even with a knife blade pressed against his eyeball Jason had denied hurting Sandie, even when he must have been in fear for his own sight and probably his life, he had denied it.

Chapter 34

"Gloria, are you there?"

"I'm here, in the kitchen. I'm making tea, do you want one? You can tell me how it went. Did you find him?"

"I have to go. I need to get away."

"What?" She stepped to the kitchen door, a tea bag dangling from her hand. "What the hell happened? What have you done? Oh Simon, have you hurt him?" She moved over to him panic and fear widening her eyes.

"No, not really, no but the police will have him. I don't know what he'll say. If he tells them it was me, they'll come here. I have to go."

"But what did you do? What did he say? Where will you go?" She was shaking her head now and reached out to grab at his arm.

"We fought, I had him, I had his knife but some busybody woman called the police. I ran, I was bloody lucky. If I'd been found with a knife – well!" He shrugged. "I'll have to go. They could be here any time. I came straight back but if he's told them – I have to go."

"Where are you going?"

"The shop, I'll go to the shop for now. It's in your name, there's no reason for them to connect it to me. If they come just tell them you haven't seen me, you don't know anything. Tell them I'm just a guest. I'll go up to the shop, I need to think." He headed for the door, stopped and paced back again. "He said it wasn't him, even when I had him and he was scared, he said it wasn't him. He said he wasn't even there. Well, of course he did. But – Christ I don't know what to think. There was something, something in his eyes. Shit."

"Go, go now. Take my car. I'll come later and bring you some things."

There was no time to speak, he grabbed the keys from the bowl by the door and ran.

His instinct was to hare up the road, get away as quickly as possible, to drive and just keep going, sod this cursed town. Just go – but then, where to? If Jason told the police who he had fought with, that he'd used a weapon, then he was marked and there was nowhere safe. He couldn't leave the country, he couldn't get a job, couldn't move around. He couldn't even risk breaking the speed limit. He thumped at the wheel. It was never ending, this torture. He was never going to be free of it, every way he turned he failed, every plan came unstuck. "Shit."

The empty rooms echoed to the thud of his feet, back and forth, back and forth. He glanced at his watch, over and over. Time crawled and all he could do was wait for Gloria. He needed her, he needed to talk to her and he wanted her to tell him what he should do, because no matter how he tried there were no coherent thoughts. Fragments of memory split by schemes and plans that got no further than the first steps. He could go to the police himself, hand himself in, go back to jail, back to where he didn't need to act but could simply plan and study and work out in the gym. Incredibly that life held some attraction. Then again, if Jason hadn't told the police who he was maybe he didn't need to run. It was possible. Jason no doubt hated him but it was certain that he hated the police, the system even more. Maybe it went too much against the grain to grass on anyone, even him. But he'd done it before. The first time. If he went back to jail to finish out his sentence he would be too old by the time he was out again. It would always be unsolved, the guilty parties would walk free and get away with it completely.

He flopped down on the moth-eaten chair, stood again and paced, sat on the floor. He went through to the kitchen and drank a glass of cold water. He washed the grime from his hands and face and constantly he grappled with confusion and panic.

Then at last he heard her rattling the front door of the shop. He ran down the stairs and gestured to Gloria to come round the back. He unlocked the gate and the door. She slid through. She had his sports bag and a carrier in her arms. She had brought him clothes and food, a flask of coffee. She climbed the stairs with him, poured them both a hot drink and added a glug of whisky to both cups.

She sat cross legged on the floor opposite to the chair, leaned against the wall. "Now, tell me what happened and then we'll see what we can do."

Calm, matter of fact, stoic.

"We fought. I didn't intend to but when I think about it of course it was inevitable. I had him though. It was his knife, but I had him. Then that woman called the police." He paused, shook his head, took a sip of the fortified coffee. "I made him go into the park. He was scared, I had him scared Gloria and even then, when he knew I could kill him, hurt him badly, he said it wasn't him. He said that he hadn't even been there."

"Well I suppose he would. He wasn't going to admit it, was he?"

"No, no – but there was something, something in his eyes. Shock, disbelief. He said it wasn't him, that he'd known her too long, that she was just a kid. He was questioned before, the police had them all in, but of course he was never accused. Why would he be? They had me. Once they found the sweater, once the lads dropped me in it they had me. Have I been wrong Gloria, all this time, all this hate? Have I been wrong?"

She watched him, silently, thoughtfully. "It was the same thing that Hardcastle said, wasn't it? That she was just a kid. I mean, I think that people who do that, hurt kids in that way – well it's in them, isn't it? A fault in them. Most men, even men like Jason, Stephen Hardcastle, they don't hurt kids, little girls."

Simon lowered his eyes, stared into the empty cup. "If they didn't do it, someone did and I have no choice now, I have to find out who and I have to find out why my so-called friends left me to carry the can."

Chapter 35

"I'm going back now, I have a camp bed, a mattress. I'll bring them when it gets dark. You might as well be as comfortable as we can make you. I'll bring the camping stove as well, it'll help. It'll only be for a day or two. If the police don't come tomorrow, maybe the next day we can assume he hasn't told them." She glanced around. "I'll bring a bucket and mop. You can start to tidy this place. It'll give you something to do. You need something to do."

"Gloria, you're amazing."

"Yeah, well." She had coloured and smiled at him. "You do know don't you, that it's because I believe you. It's because I think you've been handed a shitty stick and I want to help you put it right."

He nodded, he had wanted her to say it was because she cared, but for now just her belief was enough.

"I'll bring some fish and chips, we'll eat something, talk it out. Try to keep calm. I won't tell you not to worry but at least try not to panic. It might be okay, he might not tell them."

He wanted to leave, to go out to the moors and walk and walk until he fell into the heather or onto the tight moorland grass and then just sink down into the hills and cease the struggle. The first plan would have finished with him dead, and Gloria had stopped that. Then the second plan, the one he had bought all those stupid pills for, she had stopped that as well. But now, it just seemed too hard, an unending struggle. He could go out to the moor and leave it all but he knew he wouldn't. He owed it to Sandie and now he owed it to Gloria, she had believed him and helped him and he couldn't let her down.

She was right though, he needed something to do, something to fill these tormented hours. He went into the nasty kitchen. There was hot water and with a really good scrub and a bit of repair it could be made useable, not luxurious but functional and clean. Hot water alone wouldn't do it though, he needed cleaning chemicals. There were some things downstairs in the warehouse, he brought them back upstairs, there was bleach and soap, and in the cupboard was an old scrubbing brush.

* * *

Gloria had put a pack of lager in the carriers and he popped the top on one as he waited for the bucket to fill. It was ridiculous, housework at a time like this but it worked. As he scrubbed and scraped and cleaned, swigging the lager, he found his nerves begin to unwind. The physical activity and the satisfaction of seeing the kitchen improve was like a tiny miracle. Eventually, the light began to fade and he heard Gloria rattling at the back door. The kitchen was clean and useable, he had mended a couple of broken doors and it made him smile. He ached from head to toe but of course that was another good thing, maybe just maybe he would sleep tonight.

"Wow – that's amazing. You've done a brilliant job." Gloria beamed at him from the doorway, he had run upstairs in front of her so that he could see her reaction and it warmed him.

She turned to him now and shook her head, "Nothing has happened. No police, just nothing. So, either he didn't drop you in it or they haven't followed it up yet."

"Well that wouldn't take them long. Last time I saw Bradbury – the probation officer – I told him I was still with you, even though at the time I wasn't."

"Well fingers crossed. Come on let's have these before they go cold." She began to unwrap the fish and chips. "Have you got any of that beer left?"

He opened the last two bottles. They ate the food, drank the lager. They went over old ground until they acknowledged that was all they were doing and there was nothing further to say.

Gloria uncrossed her legs and stood looking down at him. "I bet you wish you'd never started this Simon. I'm sorry to keep saying it but the best thing would be to consider letting it go now – could you?"

He shook his head.

"Yeah," she sighed and then walked towards the door. "I'll get the camp bed and stuff. Give me a hand will you."

He caught the sadness in her eyes, but there was acceptance in her tone and he knew that she understood and, though it wasn't the way she wanted him to go, she would stick with him.

* * *

She had brought him a bed and a duvet, a pillow, a folding chair. She smiled when he looked at it.

"Well I don't mind sitting on the floor but these are much more are comfy," he said.

Once they had them upstairs she turned and walked into his arms. "I'll miss you but maybe you can come back, in just a day or two. I left some more cleaning stuff in the yard. You've made a great start though and you might just as well be useful while you wait. After all, there will be a day when this is over and you have to plan for that, don't you?"

He held her close. "You know you're the only good thing to come out of this and if it all goes pear-shaped – huh – even more, I'll still be glad I met you."

He bent and kissed her as his arms tightened round the slender body and then without another word she pulled away and clattered down the stairs. He heard the car reversing out of the yard, went down and locked the gates, unfolded the bed, threw himself on top of the duvet and let himself spiral down into the darkness.

Chapter 36

It was early when he woke, disturbed by the intermittent brightness of the sun finding its way through the clouds and the filth on the windows. Once the kettle was on, he poured himself a bowl of cereal and sat in the old chair staring outside. It was a quiet road but now and again a van or a car would pass, and the occasional pedestrian trailing towards the run-down industrial estate. It was dreary and dull outside the grime-covered glass. The kettle burbled but it was all he could manage to push up from the chair and turn off the heat underneath it. He was spiralling downwards into despair and didn't have the heart to fight it.

Gloria wouldn't come until after the breakfast service at the hotel, and probably not until she had cleaned and prepared the rooms with her young assistant. He glanced at his watch. It would be hours before he would see her. In the corner was the clutter of cleaning equipment she'd brought him to clear up the nasty, dirty room. He just couldn't find any sort of enthusiasm for sorting and cleaning, though he knew she had meant well.

He opened the back gate just a crack and peered out into the road. There was no SWAT team hiding against the wall, no armed response vehicle creeping round the corner, not even a Bobby on a bike. He shook his head. He was being ridiculous, they may have gone to Mill Lodge, they may have put out a notice that he was on the run but they didn't know about this place and anyway, just how important was a knife fight between two thugs? If he hadn't been out on licence it would have been written up and filed away but, because it was him, they would be obliged to take some action.

He turned up the hill away from town. What was needed was a long walk, to pass the hours in the open with the birds, the sky and a few moorland sheep for company. He walked quickly, testing his muscles, forcing his heart to pound and breathing to quicken. It felt good, as he knew it would and the depression began to lift as clouds dispersed and the sun came through, warm and bright. Gloria was right, this might blow over. For now, he couldn't think beyond that so he let it sit, let it be enough to have the hours on his own in the quiet of the hills.

He climbed as far as the cascade and watched the roaring water diving into the cavern beneath, endless and eternal. He could drop down there now and it would take him under and never let him go. A few hours ago that would have been welcomed but he had regained some strength with passing time. He just threw a stick in to watch it toss and whirl and disappear and then turned back to retrace his route.

There was the scream of sirens in the distance and it turned his stomach. In reality, that wasn't how they would come for him, not with noise and disturbance but quietly with stern looks and twisted mouths.

She hadn't arrived yet so he tore up the note he had left pinned to the back door, made a cup of coffee and went back to sit by the window. Afterwards he would make a start on the cleaning, after all, why not? It cheered him yesterday and it would mean sleeping here tonight would be more pleasant, if it came to that.

When at last there was the sound of her car, it was almost noon and he was hot and grubby. It had been worth it though, the room smelled fresher, the floors and paintwork were a bit cleaner and the newly washed and polished windows gleamed. He dragged the two chairs together and put an old crate from the warehouse between them, a makeshift coffee table. It was little more than a joke but he hoped Gloria would be amused and they could sit and drink tea and maybe she'd bring something to eat, a pasty or a pie. If not he'd make a sandwich with the cheese and pickle that had been in the bag yesterday.

Gloria turned into the yard, parked and before he had finished locking the back gate she jumped from the car, slammed the door and ran into the building. His heart leaped, something had happened. A shiver ran through him. So, they must have come to the hotel, he was going to have to flee after all.

He pounded upstairs and found her standing in the middle of the room. Her hands twisted and wrung in front of her, tears tracked down her flushed face.

"Shit Gloria, what happened? What did you tell them? Do they know where I am?"

She shook her head, and bent to root around in the bag that was slung over her shoulder. She pulled out a piece of paper, held it towards him.

"I printed this out, Simon. Tell me this wasn't you. Tell me you didn't do this." He glanced again at her distraught expression and then reached for the printed sheet shaking in her quivering hand.

"What, what is it?" He unfolded it and stared disbelieving at the screen-grabbed article.

Jason Parr was dead, his body had been found in the early morning by a man walking his dog down beside the river. He had been left in the little copse of trees behind where the old wire works used to be. Police were looking for witnesses. They had released an early statement because the day before, the victim had been questioned after a fight with someone outside the infant school and police were appealing to the other person involved in that altercation to come forward so that he could be eliminated from their enquiries.

Simon raised his eyes and shook his head just once. Gloria let go the breath she had been holding since he began to read.

"No, Gloria, I promise you this was not me. I was here all night. I didn't go out until this morning. Shit, I heard the sirens, I heard them."

She nodded, turned away and went to turn on the heat under the kettle as he flopped into the chair, raising a cloud of dust. His thoughts buzzed and jumbled. As Gloria handed him the steaming mug his hands shook so violently that the drink slopped over the rim and splashed onto his shoes and the floor. The air was brittle with tension and neither of them could find words to ease it.

Chapter 37

Simon was the first to speak. "It's no coincidence, is it?" They had drunk their tea silently, lost in their own thoughts. He needed to know just what she believed. "Where he was found, it means something."

Gloria nodded, but when she spoke she sounded hesitant. "I haven't had time to think about it. I was getting ready to come up and checked the breaking news, in case there was anything about you. I couldn't believe it when I saw the report. I just printed it out and came up here. I'll be honest, I half believed you'd be gone. I'm sorry for that."

He shook his head and raised his hand, let it drop back to his knee.

Gloria continued, "I am only just beginning to process it to be honest. My first thought was about you, that maybe something had happened to take you back there, to find him. But now – I just don't know what to think."

"I did go out, early this morning, I went for a walk. I needed to get out and clear my head but I only went up on the moor, up to the cascade. No, this wasn't me."

She calmed a little at his words. "I believe you but I was panicked at first. I think you're right though, what you say. I don't see how it can be chance, down there where they found Sandie. But what can it mean and what's more important really, who did it?"

"We'll have to go and speak to Hardcastle."

"Do you think? They were still in touch then?"

"Oh yes, the three of them. I saw them a while ago up by the betting shop."

"The betting shop?"

"Yes, the one up in that little block up by Hope Street."

"Really?" Gloria raised her eyebrows as she spoke.

"What? Do you know it?"

"Yes, if it's the one I'm thinking of I know it."

"You never struck me as the sort to go into those places. I know there's no reason why you shouldn't but..." Simon paused.

"No, not me. My dad, he used to manage it, for a bit – before he screwed it up somehow and ended up back inside. That was how come I moved here actually. Well me and Dave. I came with my dad, one Easter holiday. I had nothing better to do, I'd just lost my job and it was a trip out. I always liked this town. When Dave and I decided to run a Bed and Breakfast we didn't even have to think about it much, as soon as Mill Lodge came available – well it seemed like fate."

"I must have seen your dad – back then. We were always in there, did you work there then, might I have seen you?" He wondered

"No, I just came through to pass the time, I was trying to decide whether to stay around, whether I could bear to move away from Dave, it was a confusing time. I went for walks and stuff. But you, did you go in there a lot?"

Simon shook his head, "It was Jason really, I suppose he was addicted but I never had much money and it didn't appeal. That's the story of my soddin' life. If I'd had the guts to do my own thing instead of trying to be in with that gang – well maybe none of this would have happened at all." He rubbed his hand over his face, scratched at the stubble. "But, anyway that's odd isn't it – your dad managing that place."

"Yeah, that's what they say isn't it, about truth and fiction, and what is it, something about degrees of separation? So, you saw them all there together; I've no idea who runs it now, it's part of a chain, isn't it? They're still going there; blimey their lives haven't moved on much, have they?"

He shook his head.

Her voice was stronger now, surer. "Okay, so we'll go and see Stephen. Who was the other one? You said three?"

"Robbie – Robert Parker. I don't know what's happened to him or even where he lives now. I don't suppose he's still at his mum's like Stephen. He might be married. I just don't know, Stevo will though."

"Right Stephen it is then."

Simon pointed to the report she had brought, "One thing. I know they haven't a clue that it was me fighting with him anyway, according to this. Of course I can't turn myself in, not because I had anything to do with him dying but just because of the fighting. That'd be me back inside before I could draw breath and they'd think I did it, wouldn't they? They wouldn't even begin to look any further than me. God, I can't believe it, I was fighting with him yesterday and today he's dead. Dead!"

Gloria walked over and stroked his hair. "It's incredible but you're right, it means something. God knows what though."

"I think it's a warning." His face was serious, his eyes worried.

"What?"

"You know I am beginning to believe I've been wrong. All this time when I thought it was them that hurt Sandie. Jason and that lot. Well to me this just proves it probably

156

wasn't and I think that whoever did it knows what has been going on. Shit that scares me. I think they killed him in the same place as Sandie because they wanted to scare me and tell me to back off. Or, am I being paranoid, is that just too far-fetched? If that was their intention, it's partly worked. I'm scared, but I'm not backing off. Not now."

She knelt on the damp floor in front of him and leaned into his arms. For a few moments they were quiet, warming each other and gathering their strength.

"It's nasty, Gloria. It's nasty and I don't think you should be a part of it. I'm not coming back to your place. I'm staying here until I know it's safe," he said quietly.

"But, if they've been watching you, they already know, about the Lodge, me – all of that."

"It's a hotel, why would they think I'm anything more than a guest. I know we went out for that meal – my God that seems like a long time ago now. But, anyway I just think it's safer for you if I'm here. I've got to go through to Leeds this afternoon. I'll tell them at the probation service that I've moved into my own place. I'll have to go or the police'll come to you and it could all come unravelled."

"Are you sure?"

"Yeah, I'll say I'm renting it from you and, if it's okay, I'll ask them to keep calling you with the appointment times. Seems as though they just please themselves about that. Will you let me know, if they ring?"

"Yeah, course I will but what's your thinking, about being my tenant? I don't really understand."

"They'll want to know how I managed to get a contract without any input from them. It'll ring alarm bells probably. I'll tell them I was being a bit sentimental and you needed a tenant."

"What?

"Oh, of course, you don't know. I used to work here. Way back before Sandie died, I used to work here, when it was a printers."

"Oh right. So, all that about the courses…" She tipped her head.

"Oh no, it was true. I did courses about computers, photography all sorts. That was later, at first I did some law stuff. I had an idea that I'd try to appeal, I even have a qualification would you believe – what a joke."

"You haven't!"

"Yeah."

"Wow that's impressive."

"No, not really. When you have plenty of time and it's all there on a plate for you, it's not that impressive. Plenty of people in jail do it. It's just a question of working through it and they make adjustments, if you can't attend the outside stuff. It was the Open University, I had it easy. Not like when you have to go and attend classes and get a student loan and stuff."

"No, but you did it."

"Well – yeah, alright I did."

"Why didn't you do it then? Why didn't you try and appeal?" He raised a hand to the scar on his face.

"This."

"How did it happen?"

"I was jumped in the showers. I was stabbed and slashed. You've seen the scars on my belly. I was so impressed that you didn't ask me about them."

She just shrugged her shoulders.

"Anyway, after that happened it was made clear that I had to just sit it out, keep quiet and wait. No chance of early parole. The other bloke didn't get away scot free, I hurt him and it was his word against mine. The screws didn't like 'my sort'," he waggled his finger in the air, "any more than the other prisoners did. So, I just decided to let it go, make my plans for revenge and wait. That's me again isn't it, taking the easy way out."

"You know, Simon, I wish you wouldn't say that. You've had a rough ride, you've been let down. Okay, there are some things you should have done differently but don't keep blaming yourself."

"Yes, well. Come on let's go and have a word with Stephen, see what he knows. He might be even more scared now of someone other than me. Bring that paper, I'll bet he already knows what's happened but just in case."

Chapter 38

"He's away." An old woman poked her head through the window of the adjoining property, she gestured towards the little terraced house. Simon had been thundering on the solid old wooden door and calling out, while Gloria peered through the window. They had assumed he was hiding, peering at them through the grubby net curtains.

"Stephen, away?"

"Aye, he's gone away. I'm waterin' his plants for him."

"Where has he gone?"

"How the hell should I know? Just pushed a note through my letter box. It's alright though, he does the same for me. Anyway, the note said that it'd be about three weeks. He said as how he hadn't been too well and he needed a break."

"And you've no idea where he's gone?"

She pursed her lips, shook her head just once.

"Was it yesterday?"

"What?"

"When did you get the note?"

"Oh, no, not yesterday. Day or two ago. It must have been a bit sudden but he's done it afore. Gets them cheap flights and just buggers off. It's alright for some folk, isn't it?"

"Yes, I suppose so, anyway, thanks."

"Aye well, perhaps you can stop braying on the door now."

"Right, yes – sorry."

They walked to the car and Simon cast one backward glance towards the narrow house. "So, that's that then. Now what?"

"You've no idea where this Robbie person lives?"

"No, he used to live in the council flats off London Road. But they've knocked them down, haven't they?"

"Yes, a good few years ago now. Everyone was re-housed but all over the place."

They sat in silence and felt the glare of the neighbour's eyes boring into them. They knew she would watch until they drove away. "Do you think she'd know anything?"

"What the old biddy?"

"Yeah, if she's known Stephen a long time she must have met or at least seen his mates. Maybe she knows Robert Parker as well."

"But he didn't live here."

"No, but he might have visited. I'm going to ask." She climbed out and as she walked up the narrow path Gloria raised her hand to the shadowy face behind the cream lace. The door opened even before she knocked.

"What now?"

"I just wondered Mrs erm…"

"Ramsbottom, Vera Ramsbottom."

"Mrs Ramsbottom – I'm Gloria." There was a brief nod of acknowledgement. "We really needed to speak to Stephen and I was just wondering if you knew where his friend lives. Robert, I think he'd call him Robbie."

"Oh aye, I know Robbie, do I know him as well. Your hubby?" She pointed towards the kerb where Simon watched through the passenger window.

161

"Oh, he's not my – erm, I don't think you'd know him. No, I don't think so."

"He looks a bit familiar. Anyroad, that Robert, he comes round sometimes. They sit and drink beer in the back yard in the summer, him and another tall lad."

Gloria assumed she meant Jason and was relieved she seemed to have no idea what had happened.

"I just wondered if you know where he's living now."

"No, no I don't. He used to live up near the football ground, with his wife. They had a kiddie, a little girl. But they've split now. He stayed here for a bit after, but I don't know where he might be now."

"Oh well, thanks anyway."

"You could try the canal."

"Sorry?"

"Fishing – he's mad for fishing. Down on the canal. Canal or river. Most weekends, Saturday and Sunday."

"Oh thanks. That's great thanks so much."

* * *

She sat in the car, turned the key.

"She know anything?"

"Yes, she knows him, says he's divorced with a daughter. She doesn't know where he lives now though. She did say he goes fishing every weekend but we can't wait that long, can we?"

"No."

"Look, I'll run you to Leeds. I've only got one room occupied at the hotel and they've gone out walking. There's no need for me to be back. I'll run you to Leeds and we can talk. It seems that the only option now is to try to find Robert. He might know where Stephen went, then again they may have gone together and then we really are in doo doo."

"Three weeks she said. That's a long time. From what I remember he never used to go away for more than a couple of days – still, times change."

162

"You still have the other choice Simon, don't forget you always have the other choice."

"What's that?"

"You can just leave it. Nobody seems to know that it was you fighting with Jason, he's dead now. You beat up Stephen." She raised a hand to stop him as he began to speak. "You did, is it not enough? You've almost got what you came back for in a way."

"No, it's not like that now though is it. I was wrong, I don't think it was Jason and the rest at all, not anymore. I was wrong and although in a way I have got my own back for them dropping me in it, don't you see I still don't know who killed Sandie? I'm further away from the truth than I've ever been."

Chapter 39

The run in the car was very different from the desperate journey of two weeks before. Simon stared out of the window, glancing every few moments at Gloria as she in turn gave all her attention to the winding road.

He cleared his throat, "I don't think I've ever really thanked you Gloria."

"It's fine, no point in you going on the bus when we were out anyway. You'll have to give me directions when we get there. I sort of know where the Court is but I've no idea about parking. We went there now and again – you know, back when my dad and my brother were around but we didn't drive. I remember those trips back home on the bus, my mum steaming mad and me trying not to cry."

He leaned over and laid a hand on her leg. "This, the lift wasn't what I meant. Of course it's great, saves me time and it's much more comfy but that wasn't what I meant."

She glanced over at him, a crease of puzzlement between her brows.

"I meant about the other thing – actually about all of it. God, there's so much to thank you for but I was thinking about the last time I came down this road. Going the other way, on the way to the church. If you hadn't found me I would most likely be dead now."

She opened her mouth to speak but he cut her off.

"No, it's true, I was determined. Probably going about it in all the wrong way now I look back, well, see how easily I was stopped! No, but I didn't want to carry on and yet today..."

"Today?"

"Today I want to get to the bottom of it. I want to solve this and find out what happened, why and most of all who. I want to sort this and then..." He blew out the gust of a sigh, "It's hard to really explain but I actually want to have a future. I want to try and do something with the rest of my life. That's all down to you. That's what I wanted to thank you for and I see now that I can't, it's too big."

For a while they drove in silence, he didn't know whether he had offended her but couldn't see how. And then she spoke.

"You have just thanked me Simon, in the best way. You saying that – about wanting to have a future. When I first met you, I saw the past in your eyes, coming off you like a scent and I felt the tragedy in you. God, that sounds so naff and daft but it's the only way I can describe it. You scared me because I understood what you were about. If you really mean what you just said, then that's all the thanks I need. Now, stop it with all this soppy stuff, I'm trying to drive, we're nearly there. Seriously though, I know what you want but I don't know how the hell you're going to get it. Not a clue, but if I can help you I will."

The car park was full but Gloria pulled in as close as possible to the building. As he clambered out and turned to close the door she leaned across the seats. "I'll go and find a car park and have a wander round the shops. Shall I meet you in Marks, they've got a café. You really do need to get a new mobile phone by the way. But anyway, I'll see you in there, the one in the Trinity centre. You can easily take the Metro, or it's not that far to walk really."

"I don't think I'll be long, see you later." As she drove from the car park she flashed the rear lights and he saw her raise a hand. A smile spread across his face, for the first time he went into the building without feeling irritated and anxious. Briefly he wondered if it was the right thing. He wondered if it might take the edge off his resolve, then he thought of her waiting for him in the café, just waiting to sit and have a drink and then to drive them both home. It was okay, he could have this bit of happiness surely it wouldn't be a betrayal of Sandie and the debt he owed her and it wouldn't interfere with the job he had to do but rather gave him something to work towards, maybe something to hope for.

He waited for twenty minutes in the waiting room and then spent less than ten with Chris Bradbury. He ticked the boxes, had a quick joke about football, nagged again about signing on and that was it, over. It rankled a bit that he had made this journey for the short interview. There were other things he wanted to do, other more important things. The reasons for the meetings were self-evident but if Bradbury was supposed to do anything more than simply record that they had taken place he wasn't doing a very good job. If he was supposed to offer support and advice, then Simon was glad that he didn't need or want it.

He found the stop for the Metro and then regretted the decision when he saw how close it had been. He would have enjoyed the walk and maybe Gloria was still shopping. No matter, he would buy a cup of tea and a snack and sit and wait for her. He was enjoying himself. Apart from the brief times when they had made love and the walks on the moors, he hadn't felt as relaxed as this for as long as he could remember. It was golden.

She wasn't there but before he had finished eating the chicken and cheese panino he saw her collecting her tray and joining the queue.

She mouthed over to him, "Another drink?"

He nodded and moved his coat from the chair that he had been saving for her.

"Everything go okay with your probation bloke?"

"Yeah, waste of time really but what can you do?" He knew she understood, had probably heard the same comments from the men in her own family.

"I have a bit of an idea. It might go nowhere but it's something."

"Anything'll be better than what I've got. What is it?"

She put down her cup and swivelled on the chair so that she could look at him directly. He saw excitement in her eyes and felt a flare of it in return. No matter what she said, the fact that she was truly committed was precious to him.

"Well we need to talk to Robbie and though he has moved, that Vera woman said that he was mad for fishing. I think people who have a hobby like that stick with it. It's like a community, isn't it? They all know each other. It might be daft but…"

Chapter 40

"Hmm, it's a point but I can't think of anyone else. I remember he liked fishing, with his dad but he's dead and apart from that I don't know."

"Was he in a club or anything?"

"Not sure. I know he used to bore us stupid showing us his equipment."

"Okay, so we have nothing to work with, except perhaps waiting until the weekend and then trailing back and forth along the canal and river banks on the off chance that we might spot him."

"So, what we need is a contact, someone he might still be in touch with."

As they walked back to the carpark he took her hand and then once they were in the car Gloria pushed the key into the slot though she didn't start the engine. "Right, it's all we've got, we have to use it."

Simon nodded and she continued.

"This might be silly but there's a reason I've been thinking about the fishing. As I was walking around I went past a little shop, back down there," she pointed vaguely in the direction of the exit to the car park and beyond, to where there were narrower roads and small independent shops, "It was a mixed sort of place, fishing tackle and outdoor clothes, all that stuff and bait, live bait, ugh! Little pots of maggots and worms and it struck me that if Robert is so keen on fishing then he must buy all that sort of thing. I guess he might breed his own – God, that makes me itch but do you see?" Simon shook his head.

"No, sorry – I don't see what you're getting at."

"Okay, on a whim I went in and found the guy serving. I told him I wanted to get my brother some fishing tackle for his birthday. I told him I didn't know what to buy so I wanted vouchers. I asked him if there was a branch in Ramstone for him to redeem them and of course there isn't. Apparently, it's as I thought, just one shop. But, as I hoped the bloke behind the counter was like all these sorts – you know keen on something so wanting to let me know how knowledgeable he is. Anyway, apparently there is a small tackle shop up near the bus station. I've never seen it but I guess it'll be one like those over there, tucked in a corner. So, what I reckon is that, we can go into the tackle shop back at home and I bet he'll know Robert and he might be able to help us to get in touch with him."

"Brilliant." He leaned across from the passenger seat and hugged her. "Genius."

"Come on then, let's get a move on." She stopped and looked steadily at him. "One thing though, please promise me you won't hurt him. It looks now as though they might not have had anything to do with Sandie's death. I know they dropped you in it but give him a chance to explain. Will you promise?"

"Yes, I'm looking at this from a different point of view now. At first I wanted revenge but I want something else now, I want the truth. I want to know about all of it, not only who hurt her but why they did what they did to me. I won't hurt him though – yes, I promise."

"Good enough." She started the car and drove through the busy traffic and out onto the quieter road. "I'll need to be back by five – I've got some guests coming but we should just have time to pop into the shop if we go straight there. Are you coming back to Mill Lodge?"

"No, I don't think so. I'll walk up to the shop and stay there. I don't want to put you in any danger."

"Okay, if that's how you feel. I don't care to be honest, but if it makes you feel better, okay."

It took them a little while to find *Geoff's Tackle and Bait Shop*. They pushed the half-glazed door and it swung inwards with a jangle of the old-fashioned bell. It was small but, with the tourist trade in the summer and locals all year it was obviously managing to keep going. Even now at the end of the season the shelves were still well stocked and a place for the genuine enthusiast if the expensive reels in glass cupboards and the rods in locked racks were any indication.

The middle-aged man behind the counter looked up from his magazine as they walked down the narrow aisle. He nodded at them but waited for them to speak. They realized that he had summed them up immediately and knew they were unlikely to be customers, not even the sort who scurried in looking for wet weather gear when the clouds blew in and the sunny days turned wet.

Gloria stepped up to the counter. "Hi, are you Geoff?"

"That's my dad. I'm Norman. What can I do for you?"

"I'm Gloria owner of Mill Lodge." She stretched a hand across the counter and he shook it briefly.

"Pleased to meet you."

"What it is Norman, I'm trying to find a friend of ours." She waved a hand in the direction of Simon who was feigning an interest in some waterproof trousers.

"It's my friend's birthday next week and we were hoping to have a do. We wanted to invite some of the lads from when they were at school."

Simon turned towards her, he was worried now that she was giving away too much information, that the shop owner would recognise him, or ask difficult questions. He hadn't even bothered to glance over though – Gloria had put herself close to the counter and filled his field of vision.

"Anyway, we've lost Robbie's address. He split from his wife and we didn't like to ask her really." She pulled a face now indicating how awkward it would be to approach their friend's ex. "Anyway, he's always been daft about fishing and I know he comes in here and I just wondered if you knew him and you could help us get in touch."

"What's his name?"

"Robert – Robert Parker. He's our age, crazy about fishing. Got a little girl." She was using all the information she had in an attempt to give the impression of a recent friendship. He gave us his new address but we lost it."

"Oh aye, Robbie. Well he moved again just this last week so probably wouldn't have done you any good anyway, his old address."

"Oh wow, well aren't we lucky." They expected that there would now be a wrangle about privacy of information but Norman leaned over and dragged a dog-eared address book across the counter.

"You got a pen?" Gloria riffled in her bag and brought out a little notebook with a pen tucked in the sprung spine.

"16 Holmelea Heights. It's them new little flats up where the mill used to be."

"Oh, thank you so much, Norman. Thank you."

They walked calmly out of the shop and not until they had turned the corner did they high five each other.

"Yes! Blimey that was too easy." Simon was grinning broadly and gave her a quick hug.

"I know, I can't believe it." She glanced at her watch. "I have to go, I need to sort myself out now and get ready for my guests. Will we go tomorrow?"

"I was thinking I might go round there now to be honest."

Gloria frowned in disappointment.

"Okay, I'll wait, I'll wait till you're ready. Why don't you come up to the shop when you're free? Will you have time later tonight? Thing is, with what's happened to Jason, the police might end up doing just what we're doing. I want to get in with my questions first, if I can."

She smiled at him now. "Yes, soon as I'm sure my guests are all sorted I'll come up. We'll go together. Thanks Simon."

"Don't thank me, this is all down to you."

"Well, to be honest I feel part of it now. Is that alright, for me to say that?"

"It's great. You've no idea. After all these years on my own, it's wonderful."

"I'll come to the shop later."

As he walked away she wrapped her arms around herself. If this was going to end badly as she feared, then at least she could be there for him to help him through it.

Chapter 41

It felt different. Waiting in the alley for Stephen had been driven by darkness and anger. Simon recalled the weight of the hammer in his hand, the fizz of fury and hate in his blood and it shamed him. This though, pacing the floor, constantly glancing out of the window for a sight of Gloria in her little car, was excitement and impatience but it felt right. It wasn't good, but it was right. He didn't imagine that the meeting, if they did manage to find Robert, would be easy but it wouldn't be violent – he had promised.

He made a cup of tea and stood in front of the window watching workers trailing home. The light was fading and it threatened rain later, dark grey clouds glowering over the hills, the sky bruised and moody.

Constantly glancing at his watch had slowed time. The new guests at Mill Lodge were due round about five, they could be delayed, Gloria would need to spend some time with them. It was five now, there wasn't any point staring up and down the road but still he couldn't drag himself away.

Gloria had mentioned earlier in the day that he should get himself a phone and of course she was right. If he had one, he wouldn't need to stand here, he could have gone out, down to the pub for a beer, the café for something to eat. Anything would have been preferable to just waiting but it had been another promise so he would wait.

He threw himself down into the dusty old chair and looked around the room. His camp bed was in the corner, the sheet and duvet folded neatly on the top, an echo of the recent past.

He walked out onto the little landing and pushed open the bedroom door. It was dirty and dusty. Old newspapers were scattered on the floor. A pair of decaying curtains hung from a wooden rail. Not very inspiring but he should be thinking about the future. Now that he wanted one, now there was the chance that maybe he would have one, he should plan. The wallpaper was covered in colourless roses climbing round a bamboo trellis – it was dreadful. He reached up to where it was peeling from the wall and pulled. It came away easily. He moved to the next piece and dragged that down and the next. In no time, made easier by the years of damp, the paper lay in dirty layers around his feet. The walls looked cleaner and the room was brighter. He would paint in here and get a better bed. It had been great staying with Gloria but it had only ever been temporary and no matter what, this place was his for the year so he would make more effort.

He was so involved in what he was doing that he didn't hear the rattling at the shop door and Gloria was forced to sound her horn to attract his attention.

He ran down and let her in through the front door.

"What the hell are you up to? You're filthy."

"Bugger. I was just passing the time, trying to keep calm and – oh well look come and see."

He led her back to the newly stripped room.

"Oh right, well yes, that's brilliant. What are you going to do with it?"

"Just paint. I don't want to have someone in or anything and I can't do paperhanging but I can paint it."

x

174

"Do you still want to go up to see Robert?"

"Yeah, I was just filling time until you arrived."

"Well you'd better have a quick wash."

"Won't be long."

From the bathroom he shouted back to her as he brushed the bits from his hair and swilled his face and neck. "I guess I could paint all the rooms really, once all this is out of the way." He stopped, she stood behind him in the doorway. His face, reflected in the spotted mirror was suddenly saddened.

"What's the matter?"

"It's just so hard to think that it will ever be over. I've carried this with me for so long. I can't imagine life without it. It scares me. It's as if I've been holding Sandie close all this time and I'm scared that when we've finished with this I have to let her go."

Gloria moved into the room and wrapped her arms round him. "You will have to, Simon, you'll have to let her go but you don't ever have to forget her. What you're doing now, I know you think it's a debt but when it's paid, however that goes, you'll be able to let her go because you'll be free of that part of it."

"I hope you're right, Gloria, but it's like peering into the dark, I can't see an end."

"It'll be okay. Come on let's get on with it. Are you going to change your top, that's covered in dust?"

"Yeah, okay. Why don't you go down and I'll finish here and come round the back and lock the yard?"

After she had gone Simon stared for a minute at his reflection. For so long he had known what his life was about, how long it was going to be and how it would end. Now though it was so very uncertain but then, wasn't that the way it was supposed to be? Wasn't that more normal? He took a deep breath, grabbed a clean hoody from his bag and clattered down the bare wood of the staircase.

"Do you know the way?"

"Yes, I had a look on Google Earth. The flat isn't actually in the converted mill, it's a new block built in the grounds. Are you ready?"

Simon fastened the seat belt and nodded.

"Right. Here we go then."

Chapter 42

The block of flats was small, huddling beside the bigger development in the converted mill. It was faced with York stone and looked attractive but somehow feeble beside the real thing. There was a panel beside the front door with flat numbers and names inserted into plastic panels. Number sixteen was blank. "I suppose he hasn't had time yet." Gloria double checked the address that had been given to her in the fishing shop. "It's number sixteen anyway."

Simon leaned over her shoulder and pressed the button. The harsh buzzing told them that at least the electronics were working. There was no response. He tried again.

"What?" The voice was subdued and distorted.

"Robert, is that you Robert?"

"Who's that?" Simon tried a trick he'd seen on the television years ago.

"It's me." It didn't work.

"Me, who the hell is 'Me'. Who is that?"

"Robert, it's Simon – sorry Tommy, it's me Tommy Webb."

"Bugger off. Get out of it. I've nothing to say to you. Just go away. Leave me in peace."

"I just want to talk to you Robbie."

"Oh yeah, like you talked to Stevo. With a soddin' hammer? He rang me, you mad sod. I've told you I've nothing to say to you. I'll call the police if you don't leave – right now."

"Robbie, what happened with Stephen – it was bad – yeah I know that. I shouldn't have done that. I made sure he was okay though. You've obviously spoken to him. Do you know where he is?"

"I've nothing to say to you. I wouldn't tell you where he is even if I knew. I don't by the way, so no good coming here, asking questions. Leave me be."

Simon felt the grip of Gloria's hand on his arm, he covered it with his own and smiled down at her. Reassuring.

"I only want to talk to you. I just need some answers, that's all. I know now, I know you lads didn't hurt Sandie. But you do see don't you, you must see that I need to know who did and you know it wasn't me, I know you do. I just want to talk to you and I've got somebody with me. Somebody to be a witness, to make sure I don't hurt you. Please Robert, just let me in and we can talk and I promise I'll leave you alone after."

"I've got a daughter."

It was a strange response and Simon glanced down at Gloria, shrugged his shoulders and she shook her head in response, neither of them understanding the statement that seemed unrelated to the conversation.

"I know. I know you have. Robert, think about it. I'm sure you love her to bits, how would you feel if anything happened to her? How do you think my dad felt about what happened to Sandie? How much worse do you think it was for him, thinking that I'd done it? You know don't you, Robbie? You know I didn't do anything. All I want from you is to know why you dropped me in it. Why and who made you. Please, let us in. Talk to us. You're my last hope Robbie. We used to be mates. We started school together, doesn't that mean anything? Please."

"You're not listening to me, are you? I can't tell you anything. Nothing. I've got a daughter; I have to protect her. She's all I've got. Go away Tommy, go away and leave me alone. Let this go. It was years ago. I'm sorry about Sandie, of course I am, but if you carry on with this you're going to get us all killed. Let it go mate. Just leave us alone."

Though they rang and rang at the buzzer he wouldn't speak to them again and in the end, there was no choice but to turn and walk back to the car. As they reached it Simon turned and looked up at the front of the building. Many of the lights were out but on the top floor a flash of brightness indicated where a curtain had been pulled aside briefly and then left to fall back into place. Robert, watching them leave.

They sat in silence for a while and then Gloria spoke, "So, what now?"

"I have to speak to him, he's the only one left, Jason's dead, Stephen's gone – I just have to speak to him."

"Well, you're not going to get into that flat, are you?"

"No, I guess not. I wonder if he is still working at the hospital, he used to be a porter. He had to set off early to get to Leeds." He glanced around at the few cars parked in the small area. "I wonder if one of these cars is his. I'm going to come back. I'm going to come back in the morning, early and see if I can catch him."

"I can't come with you, not in the morning. I have guests – the breakfasts."

"I know, I know. I'll come on my own."

"Simon."

"It's okay. I promise I won't do anything stupid. I'll just see if I can see him, talk to him."

"Hang on – I just thought of something." Gloria climbed from the car and walked up and down the short

179

row of vehicles parked alongside the wall. She climbed back in and grinned at him.

"There, that lime green Corsa. Leeds Infirmary car park. How about this for a plan. You come in the morning and then watch to see if he goes. Later on, I'll take you through to Leeds and we'll catch him at work. If you collar him here in the car park he's going to run but if we catch him at work, I reckon there's more chance he'll talk to us. He'll feel safer anyway, won't he?"

"Maybe. Okay – let's give it a try. I suppose he works shifts anyway. I'll come up here tomorrow, hang around and then we'll go through to Leeds."

"You need to get a phone though. It would mean you could call me."

Simon glanced at his watch.

"Do you think there'll be anywhere open now?"

"What in Ramstone – you're kiddin' right?"

"Hmm. Okay – well I'll get one tomorrow. I'll come up here in the morning though and then come back to Mill Lodge and let you know what's happening."

"Come for your breakfast if you like."

"I don't know Gloria. I'm worried for you. I don't think it's a good idea for people to see us together. Especially now. He's scared, isn't he? He's really scared."

"Well the way I see it, if anybody's watching they've seen us now. Stop fussing. Come tomorrow for breakfast."

He smiled at her as she started the car and drove out of the narrow gateway.

"Are you going to come back now, we can have a bit of something to eat and a nightcap."

"If you're sure."

She nodded at him. "Okay. Yeah. That'd be nice. Yeah."

Chapter 43

Gloria invited him to stay the night. They had eaten take-away Chinese and drunk beer. Their routine reasserting itself quickly. The brandy in the quiet room, jazz in the background and the slow build up to love-making in her warm, clean bed was luxury hard to resist. "Stay, I'll set the alarm, you can still go up to the flats early."

"I'd love to. You know I would." Simon turned and ran a hand down her naked arm where it lay on top of the covers. "It's so lovely, you're so lovely. But I'm not staying. I'm still not sure I should even be here. I need to focus, I need to take care of you and this business. Tell you what though, I'd love a shower."

She punched his arm playfully, "You sod, you only came to use the bathroom." She laughed at the look on his face. "Oh go on, you know I don't mean it."

"I wouldn't do that Gloria, never again. I feel so guilty about doing that – early on, when I wanted the contract for the flat. I feel so ashamed of what I did."

"Well, you were confused, eaten up with anger. I can't say I like the idea and I do wish you hadn't done it but," she paused, "it doesn't matter any more. I trust you Simon.

181

I want you to believe that I trust you, I believe you and I think…" She stopped herself, turned away and swallowed the words she thought might scare him away. Time enough when the mess he was in had been sorted. "Go on then, get your shower. You're coming between me and my beauty sleep."

She turned away and stared into the dim room, listening as he moved about in the en-suite. The smell of fragrant steam and the hiss of water made her feel oddly lonely and afraid that maybe she was hoping for too much and had stepped onto a path leading to disappointment and heartbreak. She was recovering from the loss of her Dave, she didn't want to face that lonely struggle again.

"Don't get up, you look lovely and warm and comfy there. I'll let myself out of the front door."

"No, it's fine, I need to check all the locks anyway and have a quick check to see it's all tidy in the dining room."

She wrapped a dressing gown around her and walked with Simon to the door. He strode off down the drive and she waved as he reached the corner and turned out of sight. The rain clouds of earlier had dispersed and now the sky was scattered with stars. A waning moon sailed over the dark bulk of the moor. It was beautiful and she drew in a deep lungful of the moist air.

She almost missed the quick flash of shadow darting at the edge of her vision but the quiet shush of feet in the side alley had her whipping round with a quick gasp. The security light flicked on as she ran to the corner of the building and before there was even time to call out, a dark figure was over the wall and gone into the empty garden of the house next door.

"Hey, hey. I saw you. Who's there!" She heard the rustling of shrubs followed quickly by the thump of feet on harder ground. "I've got an alarm, straight through to the police. I'm warning you so don't come back." She dragged the towelling robe closer and wrapped her arms around her upper body. All the guests were in and so she flicked the locks and bolts on the doors. She muttered to herself "Bloody kids." But her hand shook as she tidied the little reception desk and she really did wish that Simon had a mobile phone. She would like him back now. She would like the feeling of safety that he brought, even though he was mixed up in danger.

She straightened her back. This was an hotel, there were other people here, she wasn't at any risk. Not from silly kids and chancers. She was tougher than this.

* * *

As he let himself into the drab little flat, Simon fought a sudden feeling of depression. It would have been so easy to stay with her, wrapped in her arms and drifting off to sleep in the comfort of her room. It would be so easy but he hadn't earned it yet. Later maybe, when he had the justice he wanted, when he had let Sandie go and maybe, just maybe made peace with this father. Then he might allow himself to hope for the comfort of Gloria.

It was cold and he slid under the cover and watched the faint glow of moonlight crawl across the walls and waited for the morning. He couldn't sleep. Tomorrow could be his last chance. If Robert ran as Stephen had, there was nowhere else to turn. Thoughts jostled for attention in his restless mind as he tossed and shuffled on the hard bed. In spite of all that had happened, he was further from the truth than he had ever been.

There were no logical explanations for what had happened. Why had Sandie died, was it a brutal rape gone wrong? There must be more to it – but what? She was young and innocent; she was straight forward. There had never been any chance that she was involved with drugs or even shoplifting and small crime like some of the bored kids in this little place. She was a good girl, had always been quiet and shy but driven by the need to race and to win. She worked hard in school, not outstanding but steady. There was no clue in his memory of her, no boyfriend, no reason. She was just dead and it was too far beyond pain to admit that maybe it was only because he hadn't waited for her and had let her down in the worst possible way. Leaving her alone in the gathering dark where she was slaughtered. If it really was just that then the chance of finding the murderer after all this time was nil.

Tomorrow was the crux of it and if that didn't work out, he didn't know what his life would become.

Chapter 44

It was dark and cold but there was still the occasional car and passing pedestrian as Simon left the shop and walked through town and up toward Robert's home. A couple of early buses swept past, grey passengers stared out at damp roads and a slowly brightening sky. As he reached the development around the converted mill the scene was more cheerful. Lights were on behind many of the windows, curtains and blinds glowed against pale walls. Steam drifted from heating outlets and now and again a figure would emerge. He kept walking slowly, up towards the moors.

The Vauxhall was still in the same space. Simon glanced around searching for a hiding place. He had no idea what sort of shift system they worked at the hospital so, in anticipation of a long wait he had brought a flask of coffee and a plastic bag to sit on but this wasn't the sort of place or the time that people came for picnics. At first, he thought there was no suitable place for him to stay without attracting attention. What he should have done was to borrow Gloria's car, he could have parked in one of the spaces and would have been warm and dry.

If he simply loitered on the pavement, or sat on the wall around the rough field that led out to the moor, he would stick out like a sore thumb.

He strolled through the parking area and glanced up at Robert's flat. Lights showed in two of the windows. That was a hopeful sign. If he was going to work this morning, then the problem of where to wait was eased.

There was a small, stone bus shelter on the far side of the road, inside was a ratty wooden bench. The floor was littered with discarded fast food cartons, the air tainted by a faint smell of piss and graffiti and scratchings in the woodwork informed the world that Syl loved Dan and Theresa was a slag and various others items of local interest. It was a glum little place but it was out of the chill wind and even if he was seen by drivers taking their cars out onto the road it would look innocent. Just some poor, car-less punter using public transport.

He poured coffee into the plastic lid of the flask and leaned against the cold wall. Dave's old coat had been torn when Gloria grabbed him in the churchyard but it was wind and waterproof so he had dragged it on anyway.

By the time he had finished his coffee, the car park opposite was more than half empty and still the Vauxhall was in its place, two slots in from the wall. It was fully light now and there were more people about, a few had come to stand near the shelter and when the Leeds bus pulled in they turned to him. Good manners dictated that, as he had been waiting longest, he should climb on board first. An old man with a tatty pair of paint splattered overalls and a donkey jacket leaned towards him. "You not getting this one? There's only the Leeds bus that stops here now. It's a long time until the next."

"Yeah, my mate was supposed to meet me. I don't want to go without him."

"Huh, some poor mate you've got there." With that the small crowd climbed aboard and the bus pulled away.

The bus had blocked his view of the car park. When it drove away he saw that Robert had come down from his flat and, as the road cleared, his car joined the light traffic heading away from Ramstone.

Simon breathed a sigh of relief. There was the possibility that his old friend was going somewhere else but the time and direction made it a good bet that he was heading to the Infirmary and work.

He reached Mill Lodge to find the breakfast service was in full swing. He stepped through the kitchen door and bent to give Gloria a quick kiss. "He's gone. I nearly missed him but I reckon he's gone to work."

"Okay. Sit down, you look frozen, I'll just take this through then I'll get you some breakfast. There's tea in the pot."

"I had coffee," he held up the flask. "I'll finish this off but I'd like a proper cup." She reached and took a white mug from the shelf beside the cooker and passed it across as she bumped at the swinging door with her behind and painted her hotelier smile on her face.

They had a bacon sandwich together, there was little to say. The young woman who helped Gloria had begun clearing the tables and stacking dishes in the machine. "Can you finish up on your own this morning, Rebecca love?"

"Yes, 'course I can Mrs Bartlett."

"I'm going out in a bit now. If you can do the rooms for me and then just lock up the back door, I'd be really grateful. I'll see you right in your wages."

"Yeah, great. No problems. You going shopping?"

"Yeah. Mr Fulton needs a new coat. Look he's torn that one. We'll probably go into Leeds."

"My mum can mend that one if you like. She does stuff like that."

"Smashing. When he's got a new one I'll let you have it. That's great. It'd be a shame to have to bin it."

"Come on then Simon, let's get on with this." Gloria grabbed her car keys and strode out to the garage. They were both on edge, if this didn't get them any information the whole thing crumbled to dust. She didn't want to think what that might mean to Simon and ultimately their developing relationship.

Chapter 45

"I googled the hospital. There is parking, but we have to pay anyway so I'm thinking it might be best to go into a multi-storey. There's some nearby. Looks as though it's huge though, from what I've seen."

"Whatever you think's best. I've never been there. My mum was in Bradford Royal and I don't remember much about that really."

* * *

As they walked down Great George Street, Simon stared up at the conglomeration of buildings. "Blimey, you weren't kidding. It's huge. How the hell are we going to find him in here? I sort of thought we'd just wander in and stroll about till we bumped into him in a corridor. Well, that's not going to happen."

Gloria shook her head and blew out her cheeks. "No, I reckon not. Let's not give up yet though. At least we should go inside."

The hospital was in the middle of its day, there was subdued bustle everywhere. Apart from the odd child the dozens of people, patients, visitors, volunteers who moved around the large spaces, hesitant or confident, diffident or self-important were all to some degree hushed.

"These places give me the willies." Gloria glanced back and forth as she spoke. "There's so much waiting around and everyone has a problem, even if it turns out okay it's not until you get outside that you really feel relieved. Hang on there a minute."

She strode across the entrance hall to a reception desk manned by volunteers, middle-aged men and women in aqua coloured T shirts. "Hiya."

She had deliberately focused on an older man, who had been winking at the passing nurses.

"Hello – what can I do for you?" He smiled at her and leaned a little closer.

"I'm meeting my cousin. He said I should wait for him in here but to be honest these places give me the heebie jeebies. I don't know how you can sit here all day. You're better than I am."

"Oh – not at all, just trying to help you know. Put something back in to society," he preened.

"Well I think it's marvellous."

"Which department is your cousin attending? He's a patient, is he?"

"No, no – thank god eh. No, he works here."

"Is he a doctor?" He looked very hopeful, he really wanted to help the cousin of a consultant.

She felt a little sorry for him as she shook her head, flipping her hair back and forth and giving him her most self-deprecating look.

"If only. No, he's a porter." She tightened her lips in acknowledgement of the lowly status of her relative.

"Oh. Well that could be tricky." He was struggling now to stay interested, he raised a hand to wave to a middle-aged woman whose bulky body pulled her nurse's top into creases and folds. "Hello Jenny, looking gorgeous as ever."

The woman gave him a quick smile and a nod, she had his measure.

"We're going to have lunch. I haven't seen him for ages, I'm so excited. I had no idea it was so big – the hospital. I don't know how you manage to keep track of where everything is." The flattery brought his smile back to her.

"Oh, you get used to it. Now then, let's see what we can do for you. Can't have you disappointed can we. Perhaps I know him. What's his name?"

"Robert, we call him Robbie, Robert Parker."

"Robbie? Yes, he's been here for years. I know him. Well I think everyone knows him."

"So…"

"Just a minute," he leaned over and picked up a telephone handset.

"Oh, don't ring him. I don't want to disturb him. I just wondered if you could tell me where I might find him – you know at lunch time. He should have remembered I can't just hang around in hospital but he's forgotten. I don't want to annoy him; I don't want to look stupid."

"Come on – I'm sure nobody could get annoyed with you." Reluctantly he replaced the handset and relinquished the chance to be her shining knight. "Best thing is to go to the main office, he'll have to clock off there before he leaves the site. Just follow the signs and if you can wait round there at about twelvish there'll be one of the blokes who can help you to find him."

"Oh, thank you so much, aren't you marvellous." She twinkled at him once more and then pattered away turning just once to give him a little wave but he had already switched his attention to a young woman wobbling on a pair of crutches and with her leg in a blue plastic support.

* * *

"Right, seems like the best bet is to hang around the main office and see if we can spot him at lunchtime. It's a long shot but all we've got at the moment."

"Right, this way then." They followed the directional signs, along the long corridors, turning left and right past clinics and waiting rooms, constantly scanning for a sight of Robert but knowing that the chances of simply coming across him were pretty remote.

"No, it's hopeless, we don't even know which hospital he's in. Look," Simon pointed to huge blue and white board. "There's more than one. I didn't know that."

"No, but the sleazy bloke in the reception in this building knew him."

"Yeah, but as he said, he's been here for years."

"What about his car, could we maybe look for that and then wait for him?"

"It's impossible, the chances of finding it are so low as to be a joke. Mind you, maybe that's the way to go. How about this, how about we park out by the turn off to Ramstone and see if we can catch him coming home."

"What and ram his car? How would we stop him? Sorry, Simon, I know this was really my idea but I think I was wrong."

"Let's just give it a go yeah. Let's go now and get something to eat and hang around for a while and then we'll head home but stop once we get on the Ramstone road. We can just watch and if we see him we'll try and stop him and if not we'll follow him back to the flats and collar him in the car park."

"I don't know, that sounds dangerous." She looked at his face, at the hope in his eyes and gave a little nod and tamped down the scared butterflies fluttering in her stomach.

* * *

"There, there! That's him, isn't it?" Gloria pointed out of the side window, her other hand shaking Simon dozing in the passenger seat. "Wake up, that's him."

"Shit. Yeah, you're right, I think so. Well, it's the same make anyway and the colour looks right, not many that colour green."

They had walked the streets of the town centre, eaten lunch in a pub and passed an hour in a coffee bar, irritating the owner who didn't have the continental attitude to long stay customers. Now they were parked in the gateway with a long view of the road. Gloria had become convinced that this plan had no chance at all of working. But, here he was, they peered into the car as it passed. There was no question, it was Robert. She pulled into the road, just one car behind him.

"What shall we do? What do you think we should do?" Her knuckles whitened, her fingers tight around the wheel.

"Let's just follow him, he won't be watching for us so it doesn't matter if you get right behind him, I'll scoot down a bit just in case."

"Then what? What the hell do you want to do?"

"Okay, okay keep calm. When we get behind him and the road's quiet, flash your lights. Try and make him think there's a problem with his car or whatever."

"Okay. If he stops what will we do?"

"We wait until he gets out and then we'll – well we'll talk to him."

"God, this is ridiculous! What the hell am I doing?"

"Now, go on, now. Flash your lights." She flicked the little black stalk over and over and when the brake lights of the car in front shone out at them they both yelled.

"Now indicate, see if he'll pull over." It was working and the two cars pulled onto the verge. Gloria turned off the engine and put her hand on the door handle.

"No, no wait. Wait until he's out. If he recognises me, he'll just drive off."

Robert watched through the rear-view mirror, he turned and waved a hand to them. When they didn't respond, his door swung open and he clambered out onto the grass.

Gloria wagged her hand, waving at him to come closer while Simon leaned into the rear, hiding his face over the back of his seat.

"What's up love?" Robert was bending low now, walking closer.

As he came alongside, Simon pushed out from the passenger side. Quickly, before there was time for Robbie to react, he flung himself towards the Corsa, slammed the driver's door shut and leaned against it. Robert turned, ran back a few paces and stopped.

"Robert, we really do need to speak. That's all, I promise you. We've spent all day trying to find you, please just let me talk to you."

The other man flicked his head back and forth, panicked and it seemed that he would run. There was a brief faceoff until his shoulders slumped as he accepted the inevitable.

"Come on, just get in the car. Sit in the back and we'll talk. Gloria's my friend, she was the woman who looked after Stephen. She'll make sure nothing happens to you."

Simon took hold of Robert's arm and led him forwards. Once he was inside, he slid in beside him and Gloria clambered back into the front.

For a moment, no-one spoke. Gloria wrung her hands together in her lap. It had worked but she didn't know that she really wanted to be a part of what was to come.

Chapter 46

Robert pushed as far into the corner as he could. "I'm not telling you anything. I should have reported you to the police when you came round my flat. Stevo, should have an' all. I told him but he's just beggared off. I'm telling you nothing."

Simon held up his hands, "I'm not going to hurt you Robert, all I want is the truth. I just want to know who did it and I want to know why I was made to carry the can. That's all, then you can go and I promise I'll never bother you again."

"Puh, you think I'm scared of you. Okay big man, so you've been in jail, I see the scars so I guess you think you're hard, well it doesn't impress me. You can't do a thing, I'm not stupid. You touch me and I report you and you'll be back inside before you can draw breath. Your lot have always been trouble. Let's be honest, you've got to take the blame anyway."

"Me? Come on, you know I didn't do anything."

"Maybe not, but you didn't look after her, did you? You went wandering off – up in the bloody hills." He was sweating now, perspiration running down the side of his face darkening the blue of his shirt collar. His hand shook when he raised it to jab a finger in Simon's direction. "Come to that if she'd not been so stupid none of us would have ended in this mess. You think you've had it bad, well what do you think it was like for us? It never went away you know. Every day knowing what we did and every day looking over our shoulders. You're not the only one who suffered. It's never going to go away so, no, you don't frighten me Tommy Webb. Anyway, if you want to speak to anyone you should be speaking to bloody Jason. Him and Sandie and you — between you, you've ruined my life. I've got a daughter and an ex-wife, okay she's no great shakes but my little girl needs her mum. I can't put them in danger so I'll tell you what Tommy — why don't you just finish me off right now because to tell you the truth it'd be a bloody relief."

The outburst drained him and as he sat with his head in his hands, his arms and legs trembling Gloria turned and looked over the back of the car seat into Simon's eyes. She frowned at him, all that could be heard was Robert's ragged breathing as he struggled to gain control.

Gloria mouthed words at Simon, "Jason — he doesn't know!"

Simon nodded his understanding and reached a hand across the space between himself and his onetime best friend.

"Robert, Robert." He shook the other man's arm. "Robert, Jason's dead. I thought you'd know. They found him down in the woods, same place as they found Sandie."

Robert rubbed his hands across his face and raised his eyes to stare across the car, he turned and looked at Gloria who nodded and gave him a small smile of sympathy.

"Oh shit. That's it then. See what you've done, this is your fault." He jabbed his finger now hard into Simon's chest. "You and your bloody sister and Jason — all of you see what you've done now. Let me out, just let me get out and get home. I need to phone my ex, she needs to go to her mam's in Newcastle. Let me out."

Simon was struggling with conflicting emotions, "I'll let you out, okay I'll let you out but first of all, you arsehole, just tell me why you said that about Sandie. How could you, she was my sister, she was a kid and somebody killed her and you sit there, you sit there and tell me it was her own fault." He raised his hand balled into a fist but Gloria reached out and grabbed it as he drew back his arm.

"No, Simon, you promised. Don't." She turned to the quivering wreck that Robert had become. "Why, why did you say that? It's a terrible thing to say."

"Aye, well. If she'd done as she were told, if she hadn't been so high and mighty none of this would have happened." He swung his head back again and spittle flew from his lips as he screamed at Simon. "Always too big for her own boots, bloody running champion – who did you lot think you were, eh? Anyway, she came unstuck big time didn't she and okay I wouldn't have wished that on her but I'll tell you no more. This lot, you lot, have cost me enough. Do what you like, it doesn't matter anyroad. Beat me up, kill me if you like, I just haven't got the heart to bother with it all anymore."

"I'm not going to hurt you, I promised Gloria, but you're not getting out of the car until you tell me what you meant. Not if we have to sit here all night and all day tomorrow."

"I'll tell you this and only this. If your sister had done as she was asked it would all have gone away. If Jason bloody Parr hadn't been such a stupid prick and a loser, and if you'd looked after your sister the way you were supposed to, we'd all have gone on absolutely fine. But that's not the way it was and I'll give you no names but I'll tell you this. Look to that bloody betting shop, look at the blood sucking evil swines that are mixed up in that and leave me to go and try to see if I can at the least look after my own."

He twisted round in the seat to face forward, crossed his arms in front of him and closed his eyes.

Chapter 47

Once Robert had clambered into his own car and sped off towards Ramstone, Gloria pulled out into the stream of traffic and drove back to town. She glanced constantly at Simon but he had his head back against the rest and his eyes closed.

"Come on, let's go in and get a drink." She had pulled into the drive and touched his hand.

He shook his head. "I can't, I can't just now. I need to be on my own. Christ that hurt, have you any idea how much that hurt. I have fought with that for so long. I know, deep inside," he banged a fist against his chest. "In here I have always known. If I hadn't left her she wouldn't have died. Simple and clear but to have him tell me like that, to have him scream at me like that – Jesus it hurt."

"I know. But, he was upset. He's upset and scared stupid."

"But it's true. I need to be on my own. I want to think about what he said, all that other stuff about Sandie and the bookies. What the hell has the betting shop to do with Sandie, with me? Yes okay, I used to go in there with them, I used to have a bet now and then, but nothing like them, not like Jason. What the hell can that have to do with all of this?"

"I don't know Simon, and I really don't see how you're going to find out."

"No, neither do I, but I will find out. I have to. I'll walk up home."

"Are you sure you want to be on your own."

He turned to look at her. "It's okay. I promise you I won't be stupid. I'm gutted, but I'm angry and I've got something now, haven't I? It's not much but it's something. I'll see you tomorrow in the morning. Don't worry. Please don't worry." He leaned across the car and kissed her gently.

As he tried to pull away she tightened her arms around his neck. "Come in Simon, don't be on your own."

But he pulled back and turned to climb from the car and, with just a raise of his hand, he walked down the path and out onto the road leading up the hill. Gloria watched him go, his shoulders slumped and head lowered.

As she sat in her little car, hands immobile in her lap, eyes staring unfocused at the wall Gloria struggled with the passion and the anger of the last couple of hours. It was frightening and confusing and they didn't seem much nearer to the truth than they ever were.

The front door opened and a couple came out. It was Mr and Mrs Allinson, her elderly guests. They were in Ramstone for a wedding at the weekend and treating themselves to a few days on the moors beforehand. They bent low and waved to her through the windscreen. She dragged up a smile and waggled her fingers at them. When Mr Allinson left his wife and made for the car, she tried very hard not to groan aloud.

"Hello Gloria, are you alright love? Only you look a bit pale. Frances said to me, *'Charlie,'* she said, *'look at Gloria, she looks a bit pale, go and see if she's alright.'* When the wife gives me an instruction, I'd better do as I'm bid." He laughed and turned as Frances, who had also crossed the little drive, leaned down to peer through the open car window.

"I'm fine, just fine thanks. It's been a long day that's all. Are you going off to have your tea?"

"Yes, we had a lovely walk this afternoon so now we're going down to The Oak for some pie and chips."

"Mmm lovely." She twisted in her seat and clicked open the car door hoping that they would take the hint and let her out. "Well, must get in and put the kettle on. I'm gasping for a cuppa myself."

"Right, well we'll be off then. If you're sure you're alright."

"Tell her about the man." Frances dug her husband in the ribs with her elbow. "Honestly, they never remember anything, do they?"

Before Charlie Allinson had a chance to utter another word his wife laid a hand on the top of the car door effectively trapping Gloria halfway out.

"There was a chap looking for you Gloria. When we came back from our walk. He was sitting on the chair in the back garden. Gave us quite a start. Didn't he give us a start, Charlie?"

"Hmm, he did. Just sitting there."

"Was he looking for a room? Did he say?"

"He was looking for you. Wanted to know where the owner was. Well we told him you were out. We said as how you'd gone out first thing. I hope that was alright, us telling him that."

"Yes, yes that's fine. Well, it was the truth, wasn't it?" She was doing her best to smile and keep her patience but she really wished they would just bugger off to the pub.

"Tall chap he was. Tall with curly hair." A nub of something between anxiety and excitement jumped in her stomach.

"How old was he?"

"Oh, I don't know, about the same as our Jim, wouldn't you say Charlie? About the same as Jim?"

"Aye, that's right, about that."

"And how old is Jim?"

"Well he's in his early forties now I should think. Do you know who it was love?"

"Can you hang on for just a second?"

"Yes, yes of course." She ran into the house, unlocked her private rooms and dashed into the lounge where she dragged open the dresser cupboard. There was a shoe box at the back of the top shelf. She pulled it out and threw the lid aside to plunge her hands into the collection of old photographs.

"Is this him? Is this the man?" She held out the small snapshot and the old people bent towards it, Frances slid on her reading glasses.

"Aye, that him. That's him isn't it Charlie. Oh so, you know him then?"

"Yes, I know him. It's my brother."

"Oh well, there we are. Mystery solved. That's nice, him coming to see you."

She managed to nod and wave as they turned away and strolled arm in arm towards the town centre.

Inside she picked up the shoe box and replaced it in the cupboard. By the time she had grabbed a glass and bottle, her hands were shaking so much she could barely remove the cork and pour her whisky. She perched on the edge of the settee, her legs jiggling up and down, turning the heavy glass round and round in her quivering hands and for the first time in the five years since she had given them up, she really needed a cigarette.

Chapter 48

She couldn't eat, although there was an omelette sitting on a plate, sad and cold. She knew she was drinking too much whisky. Her head was spinning a bit and she was jumpy and agitated. It would interfere with her sleep unless the glass and bottles were put away. Acknowledging this as a fact, she pulled out the cork and poured another generous measure.

He was back. Peter had come back. It had been a long time and it had seemed that they wouldn't ever see each other again. The thought was miserable back then but at least meant that he was away from Ramstone and the rough gang he used to spend his time with. In and out of youth detention, on probation and with a horrible inevitability, jail, sometimes at the same time as their father.

She had woven a life for him in her imagination. Down on the south coast, a wife, maybe some kiddies. A job, though it was hard to imagine what. Now he was back. She should be thrilled, excited that maybe they could get to know each other again. He was the last of the family apart from her. Okay, her husband had never liked him, made no secret of the fact that he didn't trust him, but at the end of the day he was her brother. The companion of her childhood.

It was easy to remember nights when they had sat hand in hand at the top of the stairs listening to the murmur of voices from the living room and then watching as their dad was led away by the police. He would glance up, knowing his children were there. He'd give them a grin, raise his thumb. *Everything's okay, it's all fine.* And they wouldn't see him again for months, and they would try to help Mum as she held it all together. Scrimping, holding her head high when the neighbours tutted at her and the landlord and the insurance man hammered on the door for payment.

It had been hard and through it all they had each other until the first time the police had come for Peter and after that it all changed. He ran with a gang of lads who scared her. He and his dad drank together and he slid into the life of petty crime and violence that ultimately had driven him away.

As the night drew in and Gloria lay on the settee, she let it all flow through her mind. The fear and anger, the despair that drove her mum to an early grave. She had been already gone when Dad had managed the betting shop and then lost that job and been arrested. She had never been sure why. It was soon after that Peter had left.

She placed the glass carefully on the table and took out the box of photographs. Some of them made her cry and all of them saddened her beyond belief; none of them chased away the whisky-induced melancholy. He had left just after the thing with the bookies. He had returned now. Coincidence? Must be, surely.

Her mind was spinning, she had to be up early to see to the breakfasts. Already a headache was gathering at the back of her eyes. She walked through to the kitchen and poured a glass of water and took three aspirin. As she swallowed the pills she thought of Simon, on his own in the flat.

He had promised he would be okay, promised not to do anything stupid. She sighed, at the end of the day he was his own man. If he was determined to harm himself, she couldn't be there every minute to protect him. She cared about him but he came with such baggage and trouble. Maybe after all she would be better backing off and curling into her own little life. It was hard work running the hotel, it was dull without Dave and she had been on the verge of selling up more than once but, it brought in a decent income and it was a good, respectable life. More than she could have hoped for, back in the days sitting on the top step, hand in hand with Peter.

He would come back to the hotel. He wanted to see her and she tried hard to find some pleasure in the thought but as she fell, unwashed and exhausted into bed, all she felt in her booze-fogged brain was worry and underneath that, fear.

Spiralling down into restless sleep she remembered vaguely that she hadn't checked the locks and hadn't turned on the alarm. For a moment she panicked. She should get up; it was important – the insurance would be void if there were problems. The guests must be taken care of, but in the end the alcohol had its way and she turned on her side and gave up the struggle.

* * *

The Allinsons wound their way back up the hill, happily tiddly from their night in the pub. Gloria's brother was sitting on the wall smoking a cigarette.

"Evening young man." Charlie held out his hand but turned away with a shrug when the courtesy was ignored. They made their way down the path and let themselves into the warmth of Mill Lodge. "Should we lock it, Frances?"

"How do you mean?"

"Well he's out there on the wall, will it look rude if we lock the door. He was just having a smoke. He must have seen Gloria."

"He was rude to you, Charlie. I don't like that. Gloria will have given him a key anyway. No, lock it – we should."

In the darkness of her room, drifting into oblivion Gloria was vaguely aware of the sound of the lock on the front door. Her mind settled, it was okay, it was all locked up and safe.

Chapter 49

He had made no noise. Before she opened her eyes, Gloria knew there was someone in the room. She was scared stupid but her head pounded and her mouth felt vile. For a fraction of a second she wondered – if she didn't move, if she kept her eyes closed, maybe it would all go away and leave her in peace.

"You awake then?" She recognised his voice immediately and her heart jumped. She forced open her eyelids and groaned.

"Peter, Peter. Shit is that you?" It was a stupid thing to say but her brain was taking time to catch up with her waking body. She tried to push upwards and nausea flooded her mouth with saliva. "Oh shit."

"Nice, that's really nice. After all these years that's the greeting I get."

"No, no – sorry. God, I feel awful. I'm not well."

"No! I wonder why that is? Oh, maybe it's the empty bottle in the kitchen, d'ya think?"

It hadn't started well. She hadn't ever expected to see him again but now and then had imagined a meeting. Maybe in a restaurant, at his new home – wherever that was. Maybe as a surprise in a public place but never this. She had never thought that he might be sitting on her bedroom chair, the light outside slowly moving through grey to pink, with her fighting to keep her stomach from revolting. If it hadn't been for the Allinsons, she would have been more shocked but she hadn't expected him to come in like this.

"Just give me a minute Pete, please. I've been stupid, drank too much. I'm so sorry. Just give me a minute and I'll get up." He didn't move but gazed around the room.

"Nice this, Gloria. Who would have imagined you'd end up a business woman, a property owner? Course I suppose a lot of it comes down to your hubby – what's his name? Oh yeah, Dave."

She still felt sick and her head pounded, this was very far from the joyful reunion she had hoped might one day happen. He leaned back and crossed his legs.

"Peter, please – could you go through to the other room? Would you mind? I'll get up, make us coffee. Would you like something to eat? I can make you some bacon and eggs. Just go and sit through there," she pointed through the door. "Go and sit in the lounge, give me time to get up. I'm so glad to see you. It's amazing."

He stood now and she slid across the bed but before there was time to swing her legs round he had crossed the room and sat down pinning her under the duvet. He leaned over and took a lock of her hair in his fingers. "Hmm, you've worn well, Sis. No grey, or do you have a bit of help from a bottle?"

She pulled away from him and the tug of his hold brought tears to her eyes. Her heart was thundering now and she needed to pee. "Give me some room eh? Just let me get up."

"Probably no need to bother yourself to be honest. I'm not staying. I was rather hoping that he'd be here but you're on your own – and just as well, I have to say. You're not looking that glam and you smell a bit rank to be frank but – never mind. I want to speak to your fancy man. I just want to know where he is."

She gulped, fear drove away all other emotion. "Fancy man. I don't know what you mean. I'm on my own. I'm a widow."

He curled a bigger clump of hair into his fingers and, as she cried out with pain and shock, dragged her head round so that she was facing him. He leaned down, close, too close. "Don't mess me about. I've seen you, not behaving like a widow now, are you? Just tell me where he is and I'll be on my way. I've been fine by the way – thanks for asking. Been back a while, keeping an eye on things. Just as well as it turns out. Look, here I am. So, as I was saying, just tell me where he is – Tommy – and I'll be on my way, leave you to your hangover and your smelly old visitors, and your booze."

"I don't know what you're talking about. You're hurting me, Peter. Please let me go. I haven't done anything, why are you hurting me?"

"Oh," he gave a great sigh and raised his free hand to grip her face, his fingers digging into her cheeks. "Gloria, Gloria, don't let's mess about. I've seen you. I've seen him. I've seen you taking him round and about in your car. The only thing I haven't been able to work out is where he stays when he's not here screwing you. I could wait, I could just watch but to be honest I'm bored by it all. I want to get back to my own stuff. I'm busy, busy – just as busy as you but not half as boring and I just want to sort this and be away from this God awful place. So…"

He dragged her head further back, the pain was intense and tears tracked from her eyes to slide down her cheeks and drip onto the creased blouse that she had slept in.

"I don't know what you want. I don't know who you mean."

She saw his fury rise, heard his breathing quicken and for the first time in her life was terrified of her brother.

She was struggling now, squirming. She brought up her hands and tried to pry his fingers away from her head. She felt hairs pulling from their follicles, kicked out with her legs but still he sat there beside her, controlling her. A smile smeared across his lips and he bent yet closer to hiss into her face.

"Fine, no probs, Sis. I can wait. I'll just sit here with you in your nice, neat little bedroom and we can wait together. I suppose your guests are going to be a bit put out when there's no nice brekky for them aren't they, but that's just a shame. Maybe they can help themselves, eh? I wonder how long he'll be. I wonder how long we'll have to sit and wait for Tommy." He let her go now, suddenly, and pushed her back against the pillow. The memory of his fingers burned on her cheeks and her scalp felt raw. He walked to the door and turned the key, taking it from the lock and sliding it into his pocket. When that was done, he sat again in her bedroom chair, crossed his legs and, taking an evil-looking flick knife from his pocket, he began to clean his nails.

Birds called across the garden and as the sun struggled to break through thin grey cloud she heard him humming to himself in the quiet bedroom.

Chapter 50

"Peter, what's all this about?" Gloria spoke quietly, her head pounded. If she didn't make it out of bed soon her bladder would let her down. For a moment, she thought of Stephen Hardcastle, how long had he struggled to maintain his dignity? How long could she?

"I need to wee." He looked up at her and waved a hand in the direction of the en-suite. She pulled her clothes into some sort of order and slid gingerly from the bed. Holding her pounding head as still as possible, she crept to the bathroom.

Though she searched desperately there was no help for her in the little space. It had been built into the alcove under the staircase of the main house and there was no window. Ventilation was served by an automatic fan and as it clicked into use, the sound of humming drilled through her brain.

Once she had relieved herself she peeled off the dishevelled clothes and wrapped herself in the softness of her pyjamas and a towelling robe. It felt better to be relatively clean. With as little noise as possible she opened the wall cabinet, there was nothing obvious to help her, no blade, no scissors, nothing heavy enough to use as any sort of club. There was however a new aerosol can of hair spray, she took it down and discarded the top, then slid it into a pocket.

A quick swill with cold water and two glasses gulped down with three aspirins and there was no further excuse to stay there. She could lock the door and sit in the quiet but what would it gain her? He would still be there and his patience would run out soon, and there was no telling what he might do then.

She straightened her spine and went back into the bedroom. He was slouched in the same position and lazily raised his eyes to where she stood in front of him.

He didn't speak.

There was nothing there of the small boy she had known, the anger that had burned in his youth had hardened his eyes and set his mouth in a grim line. She didn't like this person but there would be time enough to grieve for the loss later. For now, all that mattered was to get him away. She had her guests to consider and though it seemed ludicrous to be considering toast and bacon at a time like this, it was there as part of the whole mess.

"I need to see to the guests, Peter. If I don't they'll come knocking on the door. You know how old people panic when things don't work the way they're expecting."

He pursed his lips and glanced at his watch. For a moment hope flared, he nodded, it seemed that he would relent. Once she was out of this room it would all become manageable. He gave her a wry smile and shook his head. "Nah – they'll just mutter about it and go down to the cafe."

She perched on the end of the bed, kept eye contact with him. "I don't understand this, Peter. Why do you need to get to Si... Tommy? What has he to do with you? You've never even met him, have you?"

He didn't answer. She wanted to shake him. Where did he find this ability to be unmoved and untouched? It was chilling.

"Look, I promise you if you let me go out and do the breakfasts I won't tell anyone you're here. I won't try and run – nothing. You can stay here, have some coffee, I'll bring you a bacon sandwich. You always loved them as a kid. Thick bread, tomato sauce. Yeah? Then we'll talk, we'll sort all this out. He's not coming today anyway. I don't know when he'll come again. We had a row."

He laughed. "You never could lie very well. You've not improved."

Before she could respond they heard a knock on the door. Gloria glanced at the clock on her bedside table. Seven thirty.

"That'll be my assistant." She could see the tiny doubt. Rebecca only came for a few hours, possibly he had never seen her. It all depended on when he had watched and for how long. The idea of him observing her secretly horrified her. She remembered the night when there had been someone in the side alley, someone who ran and made off over the wall. That made sense now. The knock sounded again. Gloria moved towards the bedroom door.

"No," he had thrown off the relaxed pose very quickly and now thrust himself between her and escape from the bedroom. "Right, you don't open up. You tell her you're ill. You tell her to manage without you. Don't try anything clever."

He raised the knife in front of her eyes, grabbed her arm and propelled her through the short hall and dragged her to stand in front of him facing the door.

"Hello?"

"It's me, Mrs Bartlett."

He squeezed her arm, his finger ends digging painfully into the soft flesh above her elbow. The knife glinted before her eyes.

"Rebecca. Sorry love, I'm not well. Can you get on with the breakfasts?"

"Oh, you poor thing. Do you need anything? Do you want me to bring you some tea?"

"No, no – I think it might be flu. I don't want to infect you. I don't want to come out and spread my germs. Can you manage on your own?"

"Yes. There's only Mr and Mrs Allinson and Mr Porter isn't there?"

"That's right. Thanks Rebecca. I'm going back to bed, if there are any problems just knock."

"It'll be fine. Don't worry, I'll be fine."

She twisted away as soon as she felt his grip relax a little, stepped from the door and flopped onto the settee. Peter sat on the front of an easy chair.

"Right, now then, it's time to move this along. I don't want to hurt you. I really don't but sometimes what we want and what we need are two different things, aren't they?"

In a swift movement, he launched himself from the seat and before Gloria had time to react he moved across the small space and, looming above her, grabbed her again by her hair. He dragged her from the seat to kneel on the carpet. She felt the prick of the knife blade against her neck. The room spun and her world darkened at the edges. For a moment, she was sure she would faint. She fought back but terror had reduced her to jelly. She felt her thighs quivering, her guts turned to liquid. Surely, he wouldn't hurt her. This was her brother, was he so far lost that he could brutalise his own flesh and blood? She felt the warm trickle on her neck and the answer was all too evident. For the first time since Dave had died she tried to pray.

Chapter 51

Simon hadn't slept. He had tried a cup of hot chocolate, the instant sort which was all he had, he hoped it would help. It didn't. He had tossed and turned under the duvet until the nerves in his legs began jumping and twitching. He paced the room, constantly peering out into the darkness where pools of orange light shimmered in the puddles on old flagstones. He dragged the couple of books from his bag and tried to read but couldn't settle his mind to it. Over and over through the endless night he wished that he had stayed with Gloria.

Even if he was wakeful, her comfortable bedroom was a better place to be as the long hours crawled towards dawn.

Eventually, he lay on the camp bed, eyes closed, and let the turmoil have its way. The pictures of Sandie, the image of Jason lying on the ground in the park and the puzzling, angry outburst from Robert. Over and over he imagined the bookies, the way it had been, not now with the enormous screens and beeping machines, but back then – twenty years ago. It had been thick with clouds of tobacco smoke, the undertone of stale beer and body odour from the men who trailed constantly between it and the pub. It had been a nastier place back then, more desperate, more depressing. But, what could it have to do with Sandie? To his knowledge, she had never been in there, it wasn't her sort of place.

So, if she hadn't been in, had someone come out, had one of those stinking old blokes attacked her? The thought sickened him and when he remembered her strength, her fitness he just couldn't believe it. She could outrun any of them for a start and apart from that the place was closed by the time she finished her training. True one of them could have lain in wait but why, why her?

No, that wasn't it.

At last he heard the swish of tyres on the road and the rumble of the first buses and he got up from the bed and made a cup of coffee. Yesterday he had been optimistic but the night had driven away hope. The betting shop wasn't what it used to be, many of the punters were the sons and grandsons of the people he had seen there, and now with Jason dead and Stephen's whereabouts unknown, the whole thing seemed hopeless.

He would go and talk to Gloria. She was his lifeline and although she couldn't shed any light on what might have happened, she would listen and encourage and most of all she believed in him.

He had a wash and looked around at the dingy place. He hadn't yet sorted the bathroom but in the next couple of weeks he would buy a mixer tap and fit a shower. He needed to make his living space better, he needed to find some pride in himself and some dignity. It might help when he had to face the growing inevitability that he was never going to solve his problem. He would go to his grave without avenging the wrong done to his family. He sat in the chair to drink his coffee. Failure might have to be dealt with but it wasn't time to give up, not yet, even though nothing made any sense and the tunnel in front of him was narrowing and the light retreating.

He poured the dregs into the sink and rinsed his mug, grabbed his hoody and the torn jacket and ran down the stairs and out into the damp morning.

He would go and have breakfast with Gloria and knew that again, just being with her would make it all feel better, more manageable. He thanked his lucky stars for her and the chance that had brought her into his life.

Later he would go back up to the other side of town, see if he could find anyone in the shop from the old days. It might be that it was time to reveal himself. The probation officer had counselled against it but at the end of the day they couldn't stop him, there had never been any sort of legal decision regarding him coming home. He would let them know who he was, let them know why he was there and see if it drove any vermin into the daylight.

He stopped at the little corner shop on the way. They had a small display of flowers and plants, the bouquets were not very impressive but there were some orchids in little plastic pots. He chose two and went inside to pay. He picked up the early edition of the local paper, normally he didn't bother with it but today it would be a diversion. He had a need to think about other things and give his brain a rest from his own problems.

With the carrier bag swinging from his hand he strolled on. The overnight rain had blown away and a washed golden light shone on the hills. He turned upwards and climbed over the stone steps set into a low wall. The grass was wet and the ground soggy underfoot but he could go this way to Mill Lodge and the smell of the hills, the breadth of clearing sky in front of him and the cough and scutter of nervous sheep would soothe his nerves the way it always did.

Once he had reached the top he gazed at the little town spread in front of him. He had hated it growing up, it was boring. When he had left school and started work, he hadn't minded it that much. Probably because he was planning to leave as soon as his training was over. He was going to Manchester, Liverpool maybe – somewhere else. It didn't happen and now as he looked at the gleam of moisture on the old stone and tile he realised that he didn't hate it any more. It was home, it was where Sandie and his mum had been and it was where his dad was. Maybe in the coming days he would try again. He had planned to go to him with proof of innocence and evidence of revenge but maybe all he would be able to do would be to go and try to make him believe. Just one try, one more try.

He sat on a backless wooden bench overlooking the allotments that had been there for all of his life, and put the carrier at his feet. He would sit for a while, give Gloria and Rebecca time to deal with the breakfast service. He pulled the newspaper from his pocket. Jason Parr stared up at him from the lower half of the front page. Police were still searching for his killer, they were still searching for the murder weapon; although the streets and bins around the park had been searched, the knife had not yet been found.

It shocked him, he had made an assumption that Jason had died in the same way as Sandie, battered, strangled and cast aside like so much rubbish, but this was different. He didn't know whether it meant anything but if the method of killing was different, did this mean that after all it had merely been coincidence that they had been found in the same place? It was a deserted spot after all, not quite as much these days but still quiet. Again, his brain whirled and spun with thoughts that wouldn't settle and clear. Something else to discuss with Gloria.

He turned to page four of the paper, an interview with Jason's 'devastated' parents. He'd been a good boy. They didn't know anyone who would want to harm him. They urged anyone with information to come forward. His body would be released soon but the funeral would be just for his family. There was a footnote asking that instead of flowers those of his friends who wished to might make a donation to Gamblers Anonymous. Mrs Parr had told the reporter that her son's life had been marred by his struggle with gambling. Anyone fighting addiction should call the numbers at the end of the report. Mrs Parr hoped that maybe if speaking plainly about Jason's problems encouraged one person to seek help then some good would come from the death of her boy.

There it was again. The betting shop.

Chapter 52

He pushed the newspaper into the carrier and went down the slope towards the field at the back of Mill Lodge. He hopped over the wall into the back garden and left the bag underneath the bench. Gloria's bedroom window was dark but of course she would be busy in the kitchen by now. He walked across the back of the large residences and then over the wall and onto the main road.

By the time he had climbed up the hill at the other side of town his breathing was becoming laboured and he had dragged off the windproof coat. He could see from some way down the road that Robert's car was not in the space he had used before. He had to go all the way in case the parking wasn't specifically allocated and the car was somewhere else in the area.

It wasn't and the windows of the apartment were in darkness. It was much earlier than the last time so either Robbie's shifts had changed or he had done as he threatened and run away.

It was probably just as well. He had promised to leave him alone but after reading the newspaper article the urge to speak to him again had been undeniable.

It wasn't to be, so he turned and moved on towards the graveyard, down Church Street which was growing busy now with school kids and shop workers. The betting shop wasn't open, he hadn't expected it to be but the lights were on inside and when he peered through the window he could see a cleaner mopping the floors in front of the high wooden counter. He hammered on the door and the old woman looked up. She shook her head and pointed to the sign on the door giving opening times. He knocked again.

She shook her head and came over to the window. "What do you want?" She had shouted the words to him, overemphasising in the way of old Mill workers. "It's closed, there's nobody here." To prove it she swept a hand behind her, indicating the empty space.

"I just wondered if I could have a word." He didn't know what he was doing but she was inside and this place held secrets and that knowledge alone drove him.

She looked around the empty shop as if for advice and then with an exaggerated sigh she flopped her mop back into the metal bucket and groped under her pinafore for a key.

She unlocked and opened the door just a crack. "What's the matter? Are you daft? It's shut — bloody hell lad if you're so desperate to throw your money away go on the computer thing."

"Sorry." He held his hands out palms upwards and leaned down, hoping to make himself less imposing. "I was passing and I saw you were in and I just wondered if you had a minute."

"Well I haven't. I'm busy." She took a half step backward and pushed the door closed just a little. He didn't want to scare her, couldn't push back in case it seemed intimidating. "It's about Jason."

"Who?"

"Jason. You know Jason who was murdered."

"Are you the police? You haven't shown me any card? I've already seen the police."

"They've been, have they?"

"Of course they've been, he was killed, wasn't he? Been here with their little recorders, bothering everybody, even the manager and he's no bloody good to anyone. Scared of his own shadow. Anyway, if you're not with the bobbies, what do you want?" She pushed a hand into her pocket and drew out a small black device. "Don't try anything cos I've got this and I'll use it." She waved the personal alarm in his face.

"No, honestly I'm not a threat. It's just, well he was my mate."

"Oh, well I'm sorry about that but I don't know what you want with me."

"Well, the thing is his mum and dad want to make something good come out of what happened if they can."

"Do they? Aye well I'd be hard-pressed to find anything good out of all that."

"Thing is they want me to speak at his funeral and say something about his gambling. About how it was a problem to him. I just thought if I could speak to some of the people who knew about it, but not the usual thing, not the ones he was betting with but people who knew other things about him. I just wondered if you knew him."

"Course I knew him. Him and all his cronies and I don't know as how you'd want to hear my opinion of them."

"Oh, you didn't like him then?"

"Waste of space. Just like all that crowd." As she spoke she jerked a thumb upwards and glanced towards the ceiling.

"How do you mean?"

She had opened the door more fully and leaned against the frame, folding her arms and settling in for a gossip.

"That crowd that use the top room. Dead losses the lot of them. Been going on for years, daft lads from round here and then those from Leeds."

"Oh them."

She had to believe that he was close to Jason, that he knew about his life.

"Aye – oh them. I dread to think what they get up to. Mrs Fernley, who used to do this job before me – she warned me. Molly she said, you keep your head down and mind your own beeswax and I have. Nothing to do with me that crowd. I've never even been up there, don't have any wish to either."

"No. Maybe I should speak to them, ask them about him."

"Well, I thought as how you wanted a different opinion. You won't get that from them. I've seen them, scurryin' in that back door, all hours in and out. Thundering upstairs and then the deliveries. I don't hold with drinking, never have. I don't hold with betting so much but my Stan used to like a flutter and he were a lovely man so," she lifted her shoulders. "Anyroad, I know nowt about them except what I've seen, but there's no good goes on up there."

"Did you tell the police about them?"

She shook her head.

"Mind your own business, Molly, I was told and that's what I do. I'm sorry lad, I'm sorry about your friend but I can't help you. He wasn't my sort, not at all and I'd be hard pressed to find sommat nice to say about him. No offence meant."

"Thanks, thanks anyway." Simon turned away and heard the click of the lock as she secured the door behind him.

He strode along the road and turned left down the side of the shop next door and round into the alley at the back. The numbers of the shops had been painted on the corresponding back gates. The one for the betting shop was made of solid timber and set into a stone wall over six foot high. There were two hefty locks and broken glass had been stuck into concrete on the top of the coping stones.

A great deal of effort had been taken to make it secure but he was driven now. The comments of the cleaner had ramped up his determination to find out as much as he could about this place. He glanced around. Other gates were less solid, less of an obstacle and the one for the flower shop just two along was nothing more than a flimsy collection of decaying planks.

He put his shoulder against it and it gave after just one push. He slid into the yard and then pushed the door back in place. There were bins lined up against the wall. It was as if someone had prepared the way for him.

The second yard was piled high with vegetable crates and boxes but again there was a big industrial bin against the wall. As he crept across the space the light flicked on in the back room and he dropped to his knees under the window.

Whoever was inside the shop, whistled and clattered about preparing for the day and it was surely just a question of time before he came out into the yard, either for his first smoke of the day or to open up for deliveries.

Keeping as low as possible, Simon shuffled across the dirty concrete and clambered onto the top of the stinking refuse bin. The sloping lid was slippery with the earlier rain and slime from the rubbish carelessly thrown inside but there was a bar across the top to cling onto and, once he had made it to the top it was a short stretch and an easy task to swing his legs across the top of the wall. Whoever had been in charge of security had never imagined that this way would be seen as an access, so the glass stopped at the corner, or maybe it was because it was a shared wall. It didn't matter, it played into his hands and as he dropped into the back yard and landed with a thud he felt a flush of success.

The yard was relatively clean. There were bins and oddly a couple of garden chairs. Some broken and dirty signs leaning against the building. The window was small and covered with a wire grill and the door in the corner was heavy timber with a small square of glass at eye level and this was covered in yet another grill. He walked across and put his face close but it was nothing but blackness beyond.

Chapter 53

"He's not coming. I told you, we had a row. I don't think he'll come back again." Gloria leaned forward towards her brother. She dabbed at the nick on the skin of her throat, the handkerchief came away stained but she could no longer feel blood leaking down her neck.

Peter had pushed her away from him and as she dragged herself up on shaking legs to sit on the edge of the settee, he had thrown himself back into the easy chair.

"I missed you Pete. I used to think that one day you'd ring me, or I'd get a letter. I used to think that you'd invite me to come and see you or you'd turn up. I never would have imagined this. Why are you doing this? I thought you were away from here, down south somewhere. I tried to imagine it over and over, hope that you had a family – that you'd made a good life."

He screwed up his face and snorted. "Did you? Well, as you see you were wrong."

"But where have you been? All this time."

"Where the hell do you think I've been? I've been in Leeds, I've been in Bradford. This is where I belong. What do you think I could do in the *south*?" He stood now and laughed as she flinched and leaned away from him. "Settle down, Sis, I reckon you've learned your lesson, I won't hurt you. Well, not unless you screw me around. Look this doesn't really have to involve you. To be honest I was a bit shocked when I found out he was here, talk about a coincidence, eh? I couldn't believe it when I saw you, ferrying him around becoming friendly with him. I mean him – he murdered his sister you know. Not only that, he raped her first and there you were all pally with him. I was shocked I have to say."

"No."

"No what?"

"He didn't kill Sandie. He had nothing to do with it. He's been trying to find out what happened, trying to clear his name."

"Oh right, and how do you know that?"

"Well... he told me. He told me all about it. Why are you looking for him anyway? What has he got to do with you?"

"I haven't got time for this. It's nothing to do with you – never was. You've just got yourself mixed up by mistake but now you're going to have to come with me."

"Come with you? Come with you where?"

He blew out his cheeks and sighed.

"You know what – you were always a bit of a pain, Gloria. Did I ever tell you that? Always nagging, oh Petey, don't go out with them; oh Petey, don't get involved with that. You had no idea, did you? No idea what it was like?"

"Of course I knew. I was there as well. Don't you remember, don't you remember how we stuck together, how we helped each other, helped our mum?"

"Yeah well, we were little kids then. It was easier for you, you're a girl. All you needed to do was find somebody to marry you."

"Bloody hell, Peter, that's a bit rich. What about all the visiting, picking you up when you'd been inside? All the times telling the police I didn't know where you were when I knew full well where you were and what you'd been up to. Easy! You think it was easy to watch you throw your life away, to watch you follow dad down that path? Christ, you have no idea." She stood in front of him, waving her arms, the colour flooding back into her face. The exertion made the little wound in her neck begin to bleed again and she wiped the trickle away with her fingers and then held them up, pink stained on the ends. "And this, this is what it's come to. You taking a knife to me!"

He stood to face her, grabbed her arm and spun her around, pushing her across the room. "Right, that's it – enough. You're just like your bloody husband – all this holier than thou stuff – it's crap and you know it."

"Dave – you hardly knew him."

"See, there we are again. You had no bloody idea." He was back in her face, his spittle sickened her as she felt it, the spray of it against her cheek. "Where do you think his money came from, eh? What do you think bought this place? Scotch Mist! Do you really think his half-arsed job working in someone else's pub earned him that much?"

"He had a loan, a mortgage."

"For Christ sake, how stupid can you be? A mortgage, what world do you live in? You stupid bitch."

"He did, he borrowed the money. He told me."

"He owed the money alright but it was no bloody mortgage. And then when it got too hard to pay it back, what do you think he did then, eh, your bloody marvellous husband?"

"I have no idea what you're talking about. He did all the books. I don't know about it. All I know is that he left me well provided for. The insurance, my home. All taken care of."

"No, you didn't know, I think I believe that at least. Oh Gloria, you're such an idiot, or maybe it's not that. Maybe like this with Tommy, you see what you want to see and close your eyes to the rest. Dave borrowed the money for this place, true enough but it was no mortgage. Why do you think he went in the river, eh?"

She cried out in instant anguish, "No, oh no – he fell. He'd been drinking he fell, there was an inquest."

"Yeah that worked for him didn't it, for him and for you but you should think yourself bloody lucky."

"Lucky, lucky how was losing my husband lucky?"

"No, lucky because I stepped in for you. I held them back, the people he owed money to, I held them back because you were my sister; otherwise do you think you'd still have your hotel, your home?" He flung her from him now and as she lay sprawled on the floor he dragged open the curtains to look outside. "I don't know why I bloody well bothered, now look where it's got me."

Gloria's mind was whirling, deep inside there had always been doubt about Dave's death. She had known, she had known and refused to acknowledge it and here it was, the stark, hideous truth.

"Come on, get dressed you're coming with me. I'm sick of all this – I want it finished. I have stuff to do and I'm fed up to the back teeth of this bloody place."

The fight had left her and she staggered into her bedroom too shocked for tears and dragged on her clothes. She looked at the aerosol in her pocket, what was she going to do with that, okay she could have sprayed it in his eyes, it was supposed to work like Mace, but she wouldn't, couldn't. He was hard and horrible but he was her brother for all that. She flung it onto the bed with her dressing gown.

Back in the lounge he made her sit and wait until the door slammed and they heard the old couple fussing and laughing as they set off for their walk. They heard the clatter of dishes and the hum of the vacuum cleaner. He didn't speak again and minutes stretched into an hour and more, caught in a desperate limbo, struggling with thoughts that she didn't want and the nubs of plans for escape that came to nothing as she watched him chewing at his finger nails and pacing back and forth, a bundle of anger and frustration.

Chapter 54

Rebecca knocked on the door. "I'm off now Mrs Bartlett. Are you sure you don't want a cup of tea or anything?"

"No, I'm fine thanks love. I've made myself one. Thanks so much for your help. I'll see you tomorrow."

"You sound awful, are you going back to bed?"

"Yes, I am, I'll have a sleep."

As soon as they heard the front door slam Peter wrapped an arm around her, and dragged her close. He pushed her into the hallway and down towards the kitchen. He propelled her out of the back door and across the grass, forced her over the wall and into the field and from there towards the main road. A small grey car was parked a few yards up the hill and he dug in his pocket to activate the door locks. The lights flashed their greeting.

"Where are we going? I've told you I don't know where he is. I've told you we aren't speaking any more."

"Aye well that's as may be but I can't leave you there on your own now can I, who knows what you might get up to? I need time to think. Get in and fasten your seat belt. Don't try anything stupid. You don't want to end up in the woods."

231

"In the woods. What do you mean?"

Something flashed across his face, fear or doubt or a mixture of the two. He was off balance for a few seconds. "Never you mind. Just do as I said."

He waved the blade at her and there was a choice to run and risk it all or to go along. She hadn't the energy for flight so she sat in the car and rested her thundering head. She had never felt so tired in all her life.

He drove through town, oblivious to the swirl of life around him. Apart from the few stops at traffic lights where he tutted and fumed he drove on without a sideways glance. Up Church Road and then on down Hope Street past the little row of shops. He parked in a lay-by and then dragged her from her seat.

"What are we doing here?" There was no answer as he hustled her forward and down the alley between two of the old buildings. The passage was damp with high walls on either side, wooden doors punctuated the run of stone. "Stand there."

As he dragged out a bunch of keys and opened a sequence of locks and bolts she cast about for escape but he was quick and she was scared and confused; and then he was forcing her into a small yard. He closed the gate but didn't secure the bolts before hurrying her towards another door set in the corner of the building. Lights shone from behind a metal security grill covering a little window on the ground floor but when he opened the door it was dark, until he flicked on the light at the foot of a flight of steep stairs.

He glanced at his watch and pushed the door closed but again didn't bother to reinstate the security. With a hand on her back he made her climb into the upper room.

Most of this first floor was given over to one space. The old sash windows were obscured with stick-on film. It smelled of cigarettes and sweat. There were two tables covered in green baize in the centre of the bare floorboards. Pushed into the corner was a battered wooden desk with metal filing cabinets behind it. On the floor between them was an old-fashioned safe. In the corner opposite the entrance was a camp bed like the one that she had given to Simon. A sleeping bag lay across it, unzipped and trailing on the floor. A large sports bag and a couple of pairs of shoes had been stuffed underneath it.

"You haven't been here all the time, have you?" She glanced around.

"In this shithole, what do you take me for? Sit down."

He pushed her into a plastic garden chair beside one of the tables. "Keep your mouth shut. I've got stuff to do." He turned now and dragged a laptop from behind the door of a built-in cupboard. A small kitchen unit took up the remaining corner and while he waited for the computer to boot he filled an ancient stainless steel electric kettle and dragged two mugs from a shelf. He moved aside a couple of whisky bottles in his search for the box of tea bags.

There was a small fridge and he opened that to take out a bottle of milk. He sniffed at the top and then placed it beside the kettle. "Right, when that boils you make us a brew, and watch it because it doesn't turn itself off, piece of crap."

Once he had issued the instructions he went back to the desk and began pecking away with his fingers on the keyboard.

As the kettle started to sing Gloria stepped across the room. There was a quiet hum of traffic in the road outside and now and again the sound of people passing, the thud of the door as punters came and went in the shop downstairs.

* * *

Simon slid out from his hiding place behind the old signs propped against the wall and took the couple of paces to the entrance. He turned the knob and pushed at the heavy wooden door. Lights shone from the room above and he could hear the creak of footsteps and the mumble of voices. Bracing his hands against the walls in an effort to spread his weight evenly, he began to climb.

Chapter 55

By the time he had reached the top of the narrow stairs there was quiet from the space beyond the door. Simon reached out and slowly depressed the metal handle. He pushed at the wood and it opened smooth and silent.

He leaned close in and peered through the small gap from where he could see Gloria standing beside a kitchen unit. She was staring down, quite literally watching the kettle, waiting for it to boil. He had never seen her looking so dejected. Her face was drawn and pale and a livid mark stood out on the side of her neck. The sound of a keyboard rattled above the burble of the rapidly heating water.

He pushed a little harder and at the movement Gloria turned. Her eyes widened and she raised a hand towards him and then glanced away. She shook her head.

He pushed at the door and as it swung inwards Gloria stepped backwards into the room. A male voice, slightly mocking, filled the silence. "You're early Jack, couldn't you sleep? With you in a minute. The others haven't come yet. Did you lock the back gate?"

Simon moved from the top step and out from behind the door. As he did so Peter pushed back in his desk chair and turned to greet the newcomer.

"What the hell?"

Gloria stepped between them. "Don't come in Simon, just go now. Please."

"Gloria, what are you doing here? What's going on?" Simon came further in and flicked his glance around the space.

Peter slid open the desk drawer and drew out the contents.

He stood and turned fully towards them. "Well now, this is handy. And there she was telling me you weren't friends any more. Seems like he's changed his mind, eh Sis?"

"Sis? Is this your brother? I thought he'd gone away. You told me you didn't know where he was?"

"No, I didn't. He came back, in the night. Just go Simon, please while you have a chance."

Peter strode across the floor and slammed the door. "I don't think so. Now then, I've been looking for you Tommy, oh, or what is it, Simon – very nice. Seems like you've been making some waves here and there. Course we expected it, when we heard you were out, when we knew you were back in town. Anyway, it can't go on. Sorry but we can't open old wounds now, can we?" He shook his head and raised his right hand. The gun was small and black. Gloria gasped at the sight of it pointing towards them. She grasped at Simon pulling him close. He wrapped an arm around her waist and tried to push her behind him but she stood her ground.

She wet her lips. "Peter, for God's sake, what are you doing? Put it down, please. There's no need for this. What harm can he do you? Petey, what are you mixed up in?"

"Oh do shut up. You have no inkling of what's going on here. The people that are looking to me to put all this right. The people who want him," he waved the pistol towards Simon, "out of the way and silenced for good."

"Oh Petey, don't. Don't ruin your life. You're not thinking straight. You don't want to hurt him. It's too big a step, think of the consequences, what will you feel like if you kill him? You don't want to do that."

"Too late I'm afraid — far, far too late. That boat sailed a long time ago, and you know it's true what they say, the first time is the hardest."

"No! Oh no, you haven't."

"It wasn't my fault. She brought it on herself." Simon hadn't spoken until now and when he did it was low and angry, barely above a whisper.

"Sandie."

"Hm. Sandie, stupid kid. All she had to do was let someone else win. That was all we asked of her. Shit it wasn't as if it was the bloody Olympics, just some two pence halfpenny county thing. Too much cash wrapped up in it though. She was just too big for her own boots, up her own arse and look where it got her."

Gloria felt Simon tense and as she tried to hold him back he pushed her roughly to one side and launched himself towards her brother who took a step backwards. "You bastard. You shitting bastard. She was a child."

"Not by the time I'd finished with her she wasn't."

"Oh God." Gloria covered her mouth with her fingers holding back the words of disbelief and denial. The two men were still facing off, though Peter had nowhere further to go and surely another move and he would fire the gun and devastate what was left of all of their lives.

"Why?" The one word dragged from Simon's throat was filled with hate and pain and anger, and he moved again as he asked it.

"Because she was there and because she wouldn't do as she was told. I had people after me, I had no choice and she was in the way. She could have agreed, simply let someone else win. We would have collected on the bets and all would have been well."

"Until the next time, and the time after that…" In response to the hiss of accusation Peter simply shrugged his shoulders and waved the gun again, Simon held his ground, breathing heavily, furious.

"Was Dad mixed up in this?" Gloria had to know.

"Him, shit no. He was a liability, him with his stupid, sticky fingers caught in the till, getting the sack. Why do you think I was tasked with the Sandie thing? Someone had to make amends, to keep in with the right people. What a let-down he turned out to be. Just as we had it all set up nice he ruined it."

"But he never hurt anyone, he never killed anyone." Gloria's voice was desperate now, pleading for reassurance.

"No, but then he didn't end up with what I've got. You haven't seen my place, my car. My own car, not that heap of shit I had to rent. My stuff. You think you've got it made with your crappy little hotel, you've no idea how to live. Shame really, I would have asked you out to my place in Spain but I don't think you'd like to come now, would you?"

Simon faced him now four square, calm and solid in the middle of the little room. "Jason?"

"A clean up job and a little message, shame you didn't take the hint. Pity, he'd been so useful. That's it you see. You have to know which side of the fence to be on. You get on the wrong side and you spend your whole life trying to climb back, leaves you open to all sort of – oh what – suggestions and requests."

Gloria saw Simon's muscles tense, his hands ball into fists and his back stiffen. Before he had the chance to take a step she grabbed out and with a scream dragged the boiling kettle from the work top, yanking out the plug from the socket and she flung it across the room. A gout of boiling water fountained from the spout and this was joined with a second wave as the lid flew off and Peter screamed in pain. The sound of the pistol firing in the small space was deafening and she covered her ears with her hands to try and stop the ringing.

What followed was chaos. For what seemed like an age there was just the two men grappling in the pool of water still steaming on the dirty floor, their feet kicking thumping and the grunt and gasp of their breathing and squealing. She would never forget the squealing. Then there came the thunder of feet on the stairs outside.

Gloria was pushed back into the corner by the crush of male bodies. Customers and staff from the shop, staring round at the place that most of them knew about but had never been inside. The manager and old Jack who obviously knew the place well, all of them talking at once, shouting about ambulances and guns and blindness. As she cowered against the dirty wallpaper she saw them drag Simon to his feet and then someone rushed across to hold a towel under the cold tap and dash back to her brother where he lay on the floor rolling in pain from the scalds to his face and neck.

"His eyes, put it on his eyes!"

Along with the realisation of what she had done came the blessed darkness and the last thing she saw was Simon reaching towards her, "Gloria, Gloria, hang on. It's okay, it's all okay."

Chapter 56

Before she opened her eyes, Gloria heard the sound of sirens. The room still bustled with activity and her brother rolled back and forth on the floor. They were trying to hold his hands away from his face and to reassure him but he was lost to all but the pain and the horror of blindness.

Simon was kneeling beside her rubbing her hands and speaking her name over and over. She blinked at him and as the dizziness receded she let him help her to sit.

Paramedics clattered up the stairs taking control in the way that uniforms do at scenes of mayhem and confusion. One by one people were ushered from the room until there was just the medical people, herself and Simon and a young, frightened looking bloke who identified himself as the manager of the betting office and there on the floor – her brother.

As the police arrived they had to move aside as the sobbing, groaning wreck that was Peter was carried down the stairs, wrapped in a blanket and strapped onto a narrow chair. One of the constables turned to follow them out to the ambulance.

Simon had his arm around her, he felt warm and strong and she leaned into him and closed her eyes. She knew that there would be questions, accusations and yet more questions and she had no idea how she would ever be able to put into words the happenings of the past few hours.

"It's over Gloria."

Despite the circumstances, she heard the relief in his voice and when she looked up into his face, she saw the shine of moisture in his eyes and the smile of relief and – yes – what must be a sort of joy, hovering around his lips. She nodded at him and tried to return his smile but she knew even then that an end for him had marked the beginning of something for her and it did not contain any of what he was feeling now.

They were kind to her, they asked her if she wanted to go to the hospital and when she refused they helped her to a car and took her back to the tainted safety of her own home.

Simon had also been led to a police car and before he had bent low to slither inside he turned and waved to her. He managed a smile and though she tried, the most she could do was to nod back at him.

A quietly spoken detective came to speak to her, sitting on the settee, drinking tea made by a uniformed policewoman. "Just take your time Gloria. Tell us what happened and don't worry."

"How is my brother? Is he blind?"

"We are waiting to hear from the hospital. I'll make sure you're kept updated and then when they give us the okay we can take you to see him."

"No, no, I don't want to see him. I can't."

"That's entirely up to you. What about erm –" He glanced at his notebook. "Mr Fulton, Simon. What can you tell me about him? Where did you meet him for instance?"

How much did they know? How much was he telling them? She would keep it simple and only answer their questions with no embellishment, no unsolicited information.

"He was a guest. Just the usual sort."

"Did you know who he was when you first met him?"

She shook her head. "No – later he told me."

"Why did he do that?"

She didn't want to lie but how was she to get through this without. "I found out by accident, about his sister and what had happened."

"Did you know what he was trying to do?"

"I knew some of it."

"Did he ask you to help him to trace the people he believed were to blame for his sister's death?"

"I don't remember him asking me, not really but I just did. Once I believed him I just wanted to help him. What will happen to him now? He wasn't to blame for what happened. Peter, my brother he was the one with the gun. He was looking for Simon."

It was too much for her now and she dissolved into tears. They brought her water, they brought her tissues and then they left her alone with a promise to come back tomorrow. She called Rebecca and asked her to deal with the breakfast in the morning and then when the Allinsons had gone to take no other bookings. She said that she wanted to wait until she was well again. The girl was happy to oblige especially when she was offered a nice bonus for the extra responsibility.

With that done she dragged open the sideboard and poured herself a large drink. She lowered to the chair with the glass in her hand and the bottle at her feet and drank herself into a sort of oblivion, slouched in the lounge where she had found happiness, had experienced such fear and now sat with her eyes closed as a cloud of hopelessness and depression smothered her spirit. At some point, she walked to the table and picked up the picture of her husband and hugged it to her as she waited for the alcohol to deaden her nerves and the new grief, raw and vicious, which had opened anew the once healing cracks in her heart.

Chapter 57

Simon leaned against the polished wooden rail and watched a maintenance crew dismantling the tree and trimmings from the foyer. Down below figures scurried across the polished tiles in ones and twos. For some it was just another day at work and for others it was a day that would take them from everything they had ever known or expected, everything that they thought their lives would be.

He felt the change in the air as his barrister came to stand beside him, resplendent in her wig and gown.

"It would have been nice to have got this out of the way before Christmas, but these things always take longer than we would like. Now then, there's a fairish crowd outside. If you give me a couple of minutes to change, I'll meet you downstairs and we can get it over with. I think it wisest for you not to speak. I'll read the statement, then hand over to D. I. Prentiss. The press pack will take some pictures and screech at you but we will come back in here and I've arranged a taxi at a quieter exit and we'll slip away. Is that alright?"

"Okay, yes that suits me."

He hadn't been prepared for the noise, the crush, the flashing of cameras and for a moment he was disoriented. A couple of uniformed officers held back the melee and when the furore began to settle Mrs Quin QC began to speak.

"Ladies and Gentlemen. Mr Fulton has asked me to read a short statement on his behalf. We will not be taking any questions. We are delighted at the outcome of today's proceedings and very grateful to His Lordship who today has declared that Mr Fulton has been completely exonerated of any crime in relation to the sad death of his younger sister Sandra Elaine Webb."

"Mr Fulton stands here today without a stain on his character." At this there was a second burst of flashing, some shouted questions. His lawyer ignored them and ploughed on. "Furthermore, His Lordship has thanked my client who through dogged determination and true belief in his search for the truth has been instrumental in exposing a long-established criminal cartel who are accused of illegal gambling, loan-sharking, match fixing, blackmail and other more heinous crimes. In this regard, I will now hand over to Detective Inspector Prentiss who has information for you regarding the ongoing investigation."

Again, there was the screech of voices, demands for words from Simon, even though it had already been established that there were to be none. It was overwhelming and Simon fought the urge to run as the professionals beside him remained calm and in control.

"Thank you, Mrs Quin. First of all, I would like to say on behalf of the Force that we fully acknowledge that, historically, mistakes have been made in this case. We accept responsibility for the actions of our colleagues in this and lessons have been learnt and changes have already been implemented."

"In relation to the ongoing investigation I can tell you that the net will be thrown wide across the county in our efforts to expose this widespread and evil ring. Thanks in large part to the heroic efforts of Mr Fulton to ensure that the guilty be brought to book there have been major moves forward. We have uncovered evidence of illicit gambling and corruption which have for decades blighted the innocent enjoyment of sports fans, spectators and competitors alike. We are delighted that today justice has been served and have confidence in our ability to fully investigate and to prosecute those who seek to profit from extortion, illegal betting and usury. Thank you very much for your time. Mr Fulton asks that he now be left alone to rebuild his life."

The urge to run now was driven not by the howling of the mob of reporters but by disgust at being forced to stand silently and listen to the clichéd, placatory words that were trotted out every time there was a need to cover a monumental cock up.

There was uproar, at first it was simply noise but then Simon was able to make out the odd word, a phrase yelled louder than the others. "Will you be claiming compensation? How do you feel about your sister's murderer now? Are you going to move away Simon? Are you going to change your name again?" The lawyer stepped in at this point.

"That is all ladies and gentlemen. Thank you."

They turned and climbed the steps. "One more picture please Simon, just one more!" As he turned back and gave a small wave he looked across the top of the crowd and caught her eyes. Gloria stood across the road watching. She had on a coat with a huge hood pulled forward to hide her face but he would have known her anywhere.

He had seen her at Peter's committal hearing. She sat a little in front of him to one side on the hard, wooden benches. Her face was largely hidden behind dark glasses in a strange parody of the ones her brother had been allowed to wear to protect his still recovering eyes from the bright lights. If she was aware of him she had given no acknowledgment.

As the lawyer laid a hand on his back and encouraged him to move through the grand entrance he turned again and watched as she walked away, her head lowered and her shoulders hunched like a woman twice her age.

A taxi waited for them at the side door and they managed to slip away without further fuss. As he settled back in the artificially-scented air, Mrs Quin leaned and patted his arm. "Enjoy the moment Simon. You're a free and innocent man. I'm not saying you won't have problems, there will always be the 'no smoke without fire' people I'm afraid, but you can hold your head high and make just what you want of your life from now on. Do you know what you're going to do?"

He shook his head. "I have some ideas but I've been treading water for a while, until this was all done with. I just need time to think now."

"Well take a few days and then give me a call. You have my number and I will introduce you to a colleague who will handle things from now on."

"Handle what? I thought it was all over."

"Oh yes, but I can't handle the compensation claim, that isn't my specialty."

"No, I don't want to make a claim."

"Now, don't be hasty. This has been an ordeal I realise that and probably the thought of even more legal shenanigans doesn't seem tempting right now but you are probably entitled to quite a substantial amount." He swivelled on the seat to look her directly in the eye.

"No, I don't want compensation. I just want done with it. My sister is dead. She is still dead no matter what has happened today and no money is going to change that. I don't want blood money."

"No, no you mustn't look at it like that. It's to help you get your life back on track to help you in what you want to do next. As I say, there may still be problems."

"No. Sorry but no."

She huffed and pursed her lips. "Well as I say you have my card. If, when you have had time to reflect you want to move on with it just give me a call. But don't leave it too long, these things are better done while the state is still embarrassed and feeling guilty." She leaned forward and tapped on the glass divider, "You can let me out here driver."

As she stepped elegantly from the cab she turned again, "I am very impressed with what you did. It was brave. Now, the driver will take you wherever you want to go and don't worry about payment he's on contract." She stretched out her arm. "Goodbye Simon."

He shook the proffered hand and watched for a moment as she strode away with her briefcase swinging from the shoulder strap. They lived in another world these people and he knew from his studies in jail that it wasn't all about what they knew. He had knowledge of the same things that she did but no matter what, he would never be part of her world. He didn't have the right accent and had never had the right address.

"Where to sir?" Hmm, that was new, a cabby calling him sir, maybe some of the gloss did rub off.

"Ramstone please. The Church up by Faith Street, do you know it?"

Chapter 58

It was a bright day, the sky looked newly washed by overnight rain and the tiles and flagstones gleamed in early sunshine. Simon turned from the window and looked around his living room. Newly painted walls were clean and fresh and the floorboards, scarred and pock-marked as they were, looked characterful and homely now that they had been sanded and stained.

Physical work, cleaning and decorating had filled the days and calmed his mind as the wheels of justice had ground onward. A major police investigation had taken him in and ultimately spat him out when it became clear that he had indeed been completely innocent of wrongdoing or the knowledge of it. Hardcastle and Robert Parker were keeping low profiles, of course. He had seen Stephen just once driving his bus through the town centre and the panicked look on his face spoke volumes. The risk of being linked to the place above the betting shop scared them, hopefully enough to ensure their silence. He wouldn't ever forgive them for what they had done to him but as long as they left him alone, he would return the favour. He had pushed away the feeling of shame about the beatings and harassment, the ludicrous plan with chains and shackles. He understood that he had been driven by a hateful madness and he would be forever grateful to Gloria for her intervention. It wasn't the first or only time she had saved him and the lack of her was still hard to bear.

He had tried to see her but she had been adamant, putting down the phone when he rang and the door at the hotel had stayed resolutely closed on the occasions he had knocked. He would try again, he had to.

Nights when he might have lain wakeful in bed in his newly refurbished room had passed in the sleep of exhaustion, and days when he was overcome with frustration and fury he had left the flat and walked for hours on the moors. It was good to be alone with his thoughts and, as he had come to believe, the spirit of his sister and his mum. Just the possibility that they too had trod the paths that he followed to the waterfall and then down to the town brought them close and time and again his walks finished quietly in the churchyard with birdsong and memory that was gentler now.

His furniture was simple, a mixture of old stuff from the junk shops and some new from the Swedish place that seemed to have taken over the country while he was in jail. The moth-eaten armchair was in front of the window, reupholstered in a dull red moquette, his favourite place to sit and watch the change of light on the hills and the chase of clouds across the wide sky.

He moved through to the kitchen to rinse the mug and leave it on the new drainer. Maybe he would change the cupboards, if his offer to buy the place was accepted. Much of his granddad's money was still there and he couldn't believe it wouldn't be enough for this old place but if it turned out that way he would just renew the lease for another year. Maybe that would bring Gloria back into his circle, she still had her name on the lease after all.

It was home now and he didn't want to move. Not yet, maybe not ever. He still had to work out what to do with the shop and workshop, maybe the printing idea had some merit or maybe some sort of furniture restoration. Another course he had taken in another prison and he knew he could get more training and enjoy making old things new again.

But then, there was the other thing. It was not much more than an itch in his brain at the moment, but he had looked up the requirements on his new laptop and it seemed to be a possibility. He would think a little longer, there was time yet.

He put on his coat and grabbed the keys from the hook near the door and then picked up the tall gift bag which stood in the corner. He glanced inside. A nice bottle of single malt. He hoped it was the right one.

There was still a chill in the air but snowdrops had pushed up through the winter soil and early spring flowers in pots and planters were a promise of things to come. He walked to the corner shop and stopped to buy two bunches of daffodils and then strode on down the slight incline towards town.

He walked down Bradford Road and turned left into Mill Street. He slowed as he drew near to Mill Lodge. The No Vacancies sign was still in the window as it had been for all the winter months and now that things were starting to grow, the neglect of the garden was more obvious. There were no planters of hyacinths in the porch as with the other guest houses and care homes. No vases of tulips on the window sills and the dark windows were eyes turned in on themselves. He paused at the gate but only for a moment and then turned and moved on.

Through the town centre, and on up Church Road. As he drew nearer to Faith Street he felt an echo of the clutch of nerves in his chest but he didn't break his stride.

The creaky blue gate was still lopsided and he pulled and tugged to force it to open. He stepped to the front door and pushed once at the bell.

For a while nothing happened and he turned to look up and down the street, he saw the twitch of curtains in the house opposite. Old Mrs Denholme – still alive then.

The lock rattled and he heard the chain clatter and then the door opened a crack. Rheumy blue eyes peered out at him and then the door was pushed closed again. He heard the clink of metal as the chain was released and the door opened fully into the narrow hall.

"Come in, come in lad. Quick before the dog gets out. He's waiting for his walk."

"Hello dad, how are you?"

They didn't hug, it would embarrass them both but he held out the small bottle bag. "Happy birthday."

"Thanks son. Thanks very much." And the old man turned away before the tears could be detected.

"I brought some daffs. I thought we could take a walk later, take them up to Mum and Sandie. Is that okay?"

"Aye, aye, I'd like that. Then after we'll go and have a pint shall we, and a bit of a bite to eat maybe? I'll have to take this blessed dog out before he drives me mad. Come on in. I'll put the kettle on. It's great to see you lad. Are you well?"

"I am dad, aye, I'm very well, and you?"

"Oh aye, can't complain."

It was a good day. They sat on the bench in the graveyard and reminisced, they had a couple of pints and fish and chips. In the afternoon they took a long walk with the dog and threw the ball for him in the park. By the time he was ready to leave, Simon was sitting beside his father as the old man snored in the armchair in front of the fire. There were pictures on the mantle, Mum and Dad on their wedding day, Sandie in her sports gear and, since the last time he'd visited, one of himself, not much more than a teenager. His first day at work, he swallowed the lump in his throat and left the little house, pulling the door closed quietly so as not to disturb the dog. As he made his way home, Simon felt an ease in his soul that grew with every passing day.

* * *

It was after finishing time at the industrial estate so he was surprised to see a figure standing by the shop door. Now and again reporters had tried to get him to talk to them, offered him money and he had given them short shrift and so he prepared himself for another confrontation.

"Can I help you?" When the figure turned, it was obvious that this was no reporter; he was much too old, too frail.

"Are you Fulton, Simon Fulton?"

"I am. And who are you?"

"Clegg, Charles Clegg. I've been waiting to speak to you. I want you to help me Mr Fulton. I need you to help me."

"How? I don't understand. How do you think I can help you, I don't think we've met?"

"No, no we haven't but I've read all about you. All about what you did and how you found them buggers that killed your Sandie. I want you to help me Mr Fulton. I can pay. I can pay you for your time whatever you want, but just say you'll help me." He was going to turn the man away but something desperate in his eyes stirred up the emotion that hovered constantly just below the surface. The anger and hurt that eased but never quite went away.

"Why don't you come inside Mr Clegg? Come on in and I'll put the kettle on."

The End

If you enjoyed this book, please let others know by leaving a quick review on Amazon. Also, if you spot anything untoward in the paperback, get in touch. We strive for the best quality and appreciate reader feedback.

editor@thebookfolks.com

www.thebookfolks.com

Also featuring these characters:

TANGLED TRUTH

Other books by Diane Dickson:

LEAVING GEORGE
WHO FOLLOWS
THE GRAVE
PICTURES OF YOU
LAYERS OF LIES
DEPTHS OF DECEPTION
YOU'RE DEAD
SINGLE TO EDINBURGH

Made in the USA
Middletown, DE
16 December 2017